The Secret of Killamery

& Other Tales

❧ Flag Lane Publishers ❧

Published by:

🌿 Flag Lane Publishers 🌿

Cork, Ireland
www.flaglane.ie

ISBN: 978-1-7398589-2-6

About the Author

Vincent Murphy, a native of Clonmel and living in Cork, is a retired Chartered Engineer. As well as writing, his interests include hill-walking, sailing, travel and photography.

Previous publications:

Goodbye Kit, it may be for years and it may be forever

An imagined autobiography of Michael Kickham of Mullinahone, who in 1884 and just 23 years old arrived in New Zealand as a missionary priest. He encountered an environment uncomfortable for Irish secular priests, which led to a petition to Pope Leo XIII concerning their plight. Following a row with his bishop he moved to Sydney, getting the support of Cardinal Moran to remain there. In 1899 he returned to Ireland and in 1901 headed off for an undisclosed destination. Seven years later his family discovered he was living in Buenos Aires, no longer a priest. He died there in 1909.

Based on personal letters handed down through the family as well as extensive research in contemporary newspaper archives and Church archives in New Zealand, Australia and the Vatican.

See www.flaglane.ie for further information and reader reviews.

Conor OBrien – Sailor Extraordinaire

An account of the life of Conor OBrien who circumnavigated the globe in his own design 42′ ketch *Saoirse* 1923-1925. He was the first ever to sail a small private yacht eastwards through the Southern Ocean, and south of the three great capes: Cape of Good Hope, Cape Leeuwin (SW Australia) and Cape Horn. For this he was awarded the Royal Cruising Club Challenge Cup in 1923, 1924 and 1925.

He was an accomplished mountaineer, having climbed with George Mallory (died on Everest 1924) among others.

He ran guns for the Irish Volunteers in 1914 in an earlier yacht *Kelpie*, together with Erskine Childers in *Asgard*.

He later designed and delivered a yacht *Ilen* to the Falkland Islands / Islas Malvinas in 1926.

Ilen still sails, having been refurbished in Hegarty's boatyard near Baltimore Co. Cork. *Saoirse*, lost in a hurricane in 1968,has also been rebuilt and sails once more.

See also www.flaglane.ie

In 2011 Vincent was co-founder of *The Next Step*, a voluntary mental health support organisation based in Cork. In 2020 *The Next Step* became part of Cork Mental Health. Vincent sits on the board of CMH.

Table of Contents

The Kyiv War Museum

I

Travel to the Ukraine was in my plans for 2020 but the covid pandemic intervened and upset everything. Then it was of course Putin's 'special military operation'. Whoever did he think would believe his rhetoric on this? Of course some did, but many didn't. Sure they kept their mouths shut for the most part, a necessity for self-preservation. Not just about the war, but about everything in Russia. Only when it all ended some years back did their 'bravado' emerge. In truth I find it hard to blame them: I mean, who knows how they would react in such situations? Easy to be sure when your life, your wife or husband, your children are not at risk. Clearly there were some exceptionally brave people who put everything on the line - their lives, their freedom. Being outside Russia was no guarantee that you were safe. The Russian state security apparatus had no compunction about operating beyond its borders.

When everything collapsed and the Putin regime imploded, strangest of strange, Putin disappeared. Puff! As if he had vanished into thin air. Never more to be seen. Not in Moscow or any other Russian city, nor at his famous - or should I say infamous - palatial dacha on the Black Sea. There were a lot of investigations at the time, but mostly there was speculation and rumour mongering because nobody knew anything. There were no facts.

With the passage of time the whole Putin era has faded from the public mind. Russia is an easier place to live in now, however there remain many unresolved issues from those times.

II

So it was that last year I finally got to the Ukraine. As it's an enormous country, I think I should be a bit more specific. I spent four days on a city break in Kyiv. The city had by now been rebuilt after all the senseless and mindless destruction by the Russian invaders. It's location on the banks of the Dnipro river and its Cathedral and Churches, its historic buildings, parks and plazas, made it a delightful city to visit for a short break.

On my second day there I headed for the Kyiv War Museum, located in an old Soviet era building. A heavy, reinforced concrete building with little if anything by way of architectural merit. Functional, I suppose. However the Ukrainians had transformed the façade of the building by adding murals, flags and drapes. And there was a large plaza in front with a burned out Russian tank surrounded by a mix of traditional style and ultra-modern sculptures so that you were drawn in to the museum before ever you approached the ticket desk.

As I progressed through the various rooms, each with its own theme, I became more and more absorbed. Much of what I saw had been the subject of news reports and analysis at the time, but the museum brought it all back to life. Even more vividly than I remembered.

However, it was as I entered the Crimea room that I was stopped dead in my tracks. The attendant standing right in front of me was the head off the former warmonger and war criminal. But of course it couldn't be. He was much too young. The man in front of me I put somewhere in his mid to late fifties, certainly no more than 60. But the likeness was uncanny.

Likeness aside, I approached him for some interpretation of the exhibits in the Crimea room. He explained that initially under the Soviet Union, Crimea was part of the Russian Soviet Socialist

Republic, but that in 1954, Communist leader Nikita Khruschev gifted the Crimea to the Ukrainian Soviet Socialist Republic. This was its status at the time of the break-up of the Soviet Union. As such, there was no case to claim that the Crimea was rightly part of the newly formed Russian Federation. He was quite emphatic about this. He then went on to explain the war crimes committed by the Putin regime both in the Crimea and other parts of Ukraine occupied by Russia. All this was of course fresh in my memory from daily news reports at the time. Still, it was good to hear the detail from a Ukrainian, which was spoken with the passion of one who had suffered so much from this insane and barbaric invasion of a sovereign country by its neighbour. A neighbour that incidentally had guaranteed the independence of the Ukraine. Some guarantee!

As I was ready to move on to the next part of the museum, I couldn't help staring at this man, whose likeness to the former dictator was striking. He saw me staring, he could hardly not, I supposed. He started talking again: "You are not the first and you won't be the last to look at me and see that warmonger and war criminal. It's OK, I'm well and truly used to it at this point."

"I didn't mean to intrude on your privacy, please forgive my staring," I replied. "Mistaken identities happen all the time, there are so many people in the world who look like someone else."

"I wish it were so simple," he said, "but there is more to it than you can possibly imagine. I would like to talk to you, but clearly it will have to be after the museum closes at 6pm. Can I invite you to have a coffee or a beer with me?" He named a café a couple of blocks away. We agreed to meet at 6.30.

III

I had no idea what was happening, what to expect. I got there a few minutes early, ordered a beer and sat down. Bang on time the attendant walked in, looked around, spotted me and walked over. I invited him to sit down while I signalled to the waiter.

He was still wearing his museum name tag: V. Vladimirovich. That managed to raise my eyebrows. He noticed. Then he started talking. I became totally absorbed in his narrative. I have never before or since listened to anything with greater fascination or attention. I didn't record his story or take notes as he was talking, but I did write it down almost immediately afterwards. What follow are his own words as best I recalled.

He started: "You no doubt noticed the similarities between my name and that of a former president of the Russian Federation. This is no coincidence. What does that mean? you may ask. Nothing, you probably think, for you are looking at a 57 year old man and that criminal would be in his 80s if he were still alive.

"So let me drift back to the end of the war in Ukraine. It had been a disaster: planned on the expectation of a quick toppling of the government in Kyiv, and its replacement with a government more sympathetic to Moscow, a puppet regime if you will. But as you no doubt are aware, that failed catastrophically. Russia had some initial success in gaining control over some Eastern parts of the country, including the key city of Mariupol. That coupled with the referendum, which was admittedly a sham, gave me hope that I could secure the four eastern provinces and sue for peace on the basis of cementing that status quo. There would be some sort of security guarantee for Ukraine which would allow me to bide my time for another day. But as you know, that never happened."

My ears pricked up when he started using the first person, 'I' and 'me'. Was I talking to some delusional lunatic? I interrupted.

"Excuse me, but you just said 'I' and 'me'. What exactly is all this about?"

He nodded. "You're right, that needs some explanation. I was coming to that," he continued. "Yes you are talking to a reincarnation of that man. If I can just ask you to listen a little while longer, I hope you will understand." He was all the time soft spoken and deferential, not at all what you would expect from Putin, reincarnation or not. I invited him to continue.

"When eventually everything came tumbling down, I looked at my options, none of which were palatable. My credibility with those I had made very rich, or whose kleptocratic appetites I had tolerated, was gone. I could expect no reciprocal protection in a new regime, that is even if they themselves managed to retain some control. And as you are no doubt aware, the history of fallen leaders in Russia is not a happy one, whether in Czarist times or during the Soviet Union era. Execution would not have been the worst. As I knew only too well, psychiatric wards or the gulags were equally abhorrent prospects. My only option was to take my own life."

He remained emotionless as he recounted all this. I really didn't know what to think about this person speaking as if he were Putin himself. But equally, I couldn't stay silent about the kleptocratic nature of Putin's Russia. So I interrupted him and said: "If you really are the reincarnation of Putin, all those people you enriched, or whose grand theft you ignored, they actually immiserated the very people you were obliged to support. You had a duty to see that people's lives improved based on the proceeds of that wealth."

He replied calmly, "the Russian people would have had no idea how to manage those companies. If they were in control, in no time at all they would have run them into the ground. How could I let that happen? Better that people who knew how would run them and provide employment for the masses."

"Maybe", I continued, "but if that was your concern, then surely you could have taxed the oligarchs and provided social services to better the lives of your people?"

He responded calmly: "But that would not have restored the greatness of Mother Russia. We would have ended up a middle ranking country with no national pride or prestige. I couldn't allow that to happen."

I said nothing, wondering what would come next. I didn't really have to wait. He reverted to the topic of his own downfall.

"So I planned to take my own life. I retired to that magnificent Dacha I had constructed at Cape Idokopas on the Black Sea[1]. I went to the library which was adorned with magnificent works of art and poured myself a shot of the most exquisite reserve Vodka. I toasted the Russian flag before downing the drink in one go. Then I dashed the shot glass into the fireplace in true Russian tradition.

"I got my gun, an FSB issue Glock 17, sat down and took a deep breath. This was the only way it could end. I raised the gun, pointed it at my left eye and pulled the trigger. I heard the report but the bullet didn't come.

"Instead, it stayed just in front of the barrel, just there, floating, in an eerie and threatening manner. Was I in some sort of suspended animation? I waited for the end that never came. After several moments in this surreal existence, two hands appeared in front of my eyes and took hold of the bullet and gun. I was terrified. I thought now I was certain to spend the rest of my days in a gulag or in a mental institution. I didn't know which would be worse. Probably a mental institution. From there, there would be no escape, but they would keep me physically alive, prolonging the torture. In the gulags there would be a short enough life of torture and terror to look forward to before the inevitable relief of an early death."

---

[1] Can be seen on Google Maps, satellite view; also the subject of videos on YouTube.

He paused for a moment. He seemed to be gazing at some distant point, but in reality at nothing. He continued.

"Reflecting back now, either of those would have been preferable to what happened. In time the ephemeral being whose hands had taken the gun and bullet, revealed him or herself to me. There was no gender apparent. It - I'll use 'It' as a gender neutral pronoun, much as it pains me to pander to those gender liberals - It presented itself in front of me. I wondered what It represented. Myself, I am a Russian Orthodox Christian. You may wonder if I had any serious attachment to any religion, based on how I lived my life. But I saw the Church as an integral part of Russian identity. I had many long discussions with the Russian Patriarch, who agreed with me and helped reinforce my beliefs. I expected to be confronted by St. Peter or the Lord God himself, and I was prepared to defend my life. But this was different. It eventually spoke:

> 'Vladimir Vladimirovich, this is the voice of the Lord of Creation and of Reincarnations. You must answer to me for everything you did during your lifetime on Earth. I am sorry to disappoint you, but your expectation of meeting St Peter or the Christian God is an illusion. In the course of your life you have used your talents and acquired power to impose extreme misery on tens of millions of your own people. You enriched yourself by corrupt means at their expense, people who, as president, you were bound to protect and improve their lives. And it was not enough to immiserate your own people. You then took it upon yourself to spread destruction and misery on your Ukrainian neighbours. How do you respond?'

"This I never could have expected. Indeed I convinced myself that this was the work of the Devil, of Satan himself, trying to get between me and my Lord God. Exactly what one might expect of

Satan. I thought to myself: 'I'll have to be careful. The good Lord will surely be observing how I respond.' My first action was to make the sign of the cross and shout BEGONE SATAN!

"Little good did it do me. The response came back:

> 'Nice tactic, however that is not the world you are in. Your Christian religion provides a very good moral framework as indeed do religions in general. Humans are fallible beings and are prone to fall short of the ideal. This is to be expected. However, some people totally ignore the moral framework and indulge in horrific abuse. You are one of those and I am afraid the time has come for you to be called to account.'

"I didn't know what to expect. If It wasn't the Christian God of my Orthodox Religion, I supposed I would hardly be sent to Hell, a place that in any case I didn't believe existed. I didn't have long to wait to discover my fate.

" It continued:

> 'You are thinking about the Fires of Hell, but you don't believe they exist. In that, you are right. Some people believe in reincarnation. Yes, you will recall that I introduced myself as Lord of Creation and of Reincarnations. So you may take from that that reincarnations do happen. But it's not for everyone, just for the select few who are chosen to atone for evil deeds in their first life. You have been chosen.'

"There was nothing to say. Quite clearly a Christian act of contrition was not going to work here. So much for the Patriarch and the Russian Orthodox Church.

"I didn't have long to wait to discover my fate:

'You will be reincarnated in your own likeness but 25 years younger. Although much younger, you will still be very recognisable and will live in Ukraine amongst people on whom you inflicted appalling violence. You will work in the Crimea section of the Kyiv War Museum, where you will be reminded daily of the people you sought to colonise and oppress. All this has been arranged. You will have a small apartment, adequate but without any luxury, close to the Museum. You will live alone. You will age slowly so that there will be no question of death bringing you an early release. This life will end and you will be able to die in peace the moment you genuinely repent for your appalling deeds.'

"On first hearing, my fate didn't sound too bad. At least I could have a life of adequate comfort. I could easily brush off anyone who tried to imply I was the former president of the Russian Federation. But that's not exactly how things turned out.

"I found myself suddenly living in a small apartment a few blocks from the museum. I had a small amount of money in my pocket. There was a newspaper on the table open at a page with an ad for museum attendants. Well, I thought, I'm not going for that. The great God of whatever can go and whistle, I thought. I'm here now and I have my own free will and will make my own choices. I went to grab the newspaper to throw it away. As my hand approached it, it was as if a magnetic force was pulling it back, the nearer it got, the stronger the force, such that I couldn't do that simple task.

Then a voice came from nowhere, It was inside my head.

'Tut tut, Vladimir Vladimirovich, that is not in the plan. You will find that your free will died with your reincarnation. You had your free will and you made appalling, selfish, use of it.

In your reincarnation you will do what you must until you gain redemption.'

"It seemed I was just a marionette, destined to do what the string puller mandated, but with a mind of my own trapped forever. Such as would drive you insane. But my mind was being carefully curated to prevent insanity. Instead I am reminded day by day, moment by moment of my impotence. It is a living hell.

"I submitted my application to the museum - as if I had any choice in the matter. I was called for interview. There was no apparent recognition of who I resembled. They noted my name Vladimir Vladimirovich was Russian and asked about my loyalties during the war. Much to my chagrin, I found myself answering that I was from the Donetsk region and had been abused by the Russian aggressor, that I had been delighted to see the back of them and that I was now delighted to be back in the Ukrainian fold.

"Every day in the museum, lots of Ukrainians and others come to view the exhibition. When I hear something like 'Isn't it appalling what the Russians did?' or 'That monster Putin has a lot to answer for.' I want to attack them or send them to jail, or anything to show my rage at their idiocy and contempt. That's what they deserve. But this string puller knows how to ensure the rage bubbles within without showing any emotion. And the Russians visitors are worse. 'What Putin did in our name was nothing short of criminal. How could we have been so blind to what was going on? Special military operation? I hope he's burning in hell!' How can they not see what a disaster the break-up of the Soviet Union was? That I was restoring the great Russian Empire to give them back their pride in a great nation?"

Once more, I had to interrupt. "But surely the mark of a great nation is the success of the people? And that the state should use best endeavours in making a good life for everyone? How does invading

11

another sovereign state give you pride? What pride did the German and Japanese nations gain from their second World War conquests? Surely you as a Russian must understand that."

He replied: "But you are Irish. You must understand. Don't you want to kick the British out? We were just the same, we wanted to kick those fascists out of the cradle of our Great Russian Nation."

I agreed that I would like to see our country reunited, but only with the consent of the people. War just wasn't an option. He didn't respond.

I continued: "And what about the guarantees of territorial integrity if Ukraine returned its nuclear weapons to Russia? Did that have any meaning?"

He cut this short, saying: "Ask Yeltsin. Nothing to do with me."

He continued: "Today when you came to the Crimea exhibition, my first reaction was 'does this idiot not realise that the Crimea always was and always will be part of the soul of the Russian Motherland?' I just wanted to scream at the international consensus that the Crimea is Ukrainian. If it wasn't for that imbecile Khruschev, a Ukrainian, 'gifting' it to the Ukraine in 1954, it would have remained Russian even after the disintegration of the Soviet Union. Khruschev was a minnow, he even backed down on Cuba. He didn't have the guts to finish what he started."

At this point I interrupted again. "But actually Khruschev did get a quid pro quo when he got the Americans to remove missiles from Turkey. Surely a win for him."

"You may think that," he replied, "but he was so weak, he even agreed to keep that small concession a secret so that the GREAT USA could boast that they got the Soviet Union to back down. Kennedy needed a win after the Bay of Pigs fiasco and Khruschev handed it to him without a protest."

All this time he spoke in a voice more akin to someone telling stories to children. His words and his demeanour did not at all match. He sensed what I was thinking.

"You are wondering how I can be so softly spoken with such words of obvious passion. This is part of my living hell. The Lord of whatever is inside my head, managing how I say everything. I must talk at all times with a quiet friendly voice and demeanour. You have no idea how it makes you feel to have to play such games. When I try to match my voice to my inner feelings, this so-called Lord of Creation and Reincarnations intervenes to prevent it. In the background. You would never be aware of this.

"I am unable to form relationships with other people. If I try to engage with a pretty woman or a like-minded fellow, It intervenes to prevent it. I must live a life of lonely solitude.

"While I am slowly going mad, my mind is carefully managed to keep me sane but eternally angry at the people I see and hear at the museum. I am prevented from taking that final step to insanity, which would surely bring me the peace I so passionately crave. I am in a living hell with no escape.

"Unless and until I repent for what It chooses to call my evil doings, I am destined to remain incarcerated in this twilight zone. And here I will remain until It decides I have genuinely repented. Regret for everything I did, heartfelt and unreserved. According to Its rules. There is no meeting It half way. All or nothing."

At this point he stood up. His last words were: "I regret nothing", spoken with the same calm voice and friendly demeanour he had displayed throughout our encounter.

He walked away, without saying another word.

IV

I remained seated for a long time trying to digest what I just heard. Was he delusional? A Walter Mitty character? Or had I just witnessed some cosmic justice playing out? If the latter, it would seem the reincarnated Putin was destined to remain in his living hell for a very long time indeed

An Invasion is Announced

I

As Tony later told the story, sometime in 1940 news of a planned German invasion reached the members of the Local Security Force in Clonmel, Ireland. The invasion was expected some 25 miles away at the coastal town of Dungarvan on the following day which would be the monthly Fair Day in Clonmel

But first, some context. When Britain declared war on Germany in 1939, Ireland remained neutral and declared a National Emergency. Accordingly, this period is referred to as *The Emergency*.

There was a recruitment drive to increase army numbers massively to be able to protect the country in the event of an invasion. A reserve force, the Local Security Force was also created.

Threats of invasion were real. Hitler developed a Plan Green to invade Ireland as a backdoor to England. And there was also the threat of an invasion from Mr. Churchill to take back the ports of Queenstown (now Cobh), Berehaven and Swilly which had only been returned to Irish control in 1938. Churchill promised to reunify Ireland if we backed his war effort, then threatened to take the ports by force if we didn't. However, 1939 was a mere sixteen years after the end of a bitter civil war following independence from Great Britain, much too recent for Mr. DeValera to contemplate re-opening old wounds by joining Mr. Churchill.

II

And well you may ask, what exactly was a Fair Day? This was a monthly event in the calendar of many an Irish town until sometime in the 1960s, where cattle were bought and sold on the streets. Later, the new cattle marts being built across Ireland, together with increased road traffic, drew the buying and selling of cattle away from the streets of Irish towns. The old dispensation gave way to the new.

But back in 1940, the Fair Day was in its prime. Clonmel was no exception and on the first Wednesday of each month all the farmers for miles around with beasts to sell, would drive their cattle to town. Others would go to town with the intention of buying some animals – if the price was right.

Then there were the tanglers, those middle men of the deal. They never owned any animals, but they had a keen sense of the their value and were good judges of how much a farmer might accept. If the tangler felt he could get a better price himself later, he would do a deal. And the farmer, well pleased that early in the day he had sold for an acceptable price, could now go and enjoy the rest of the day, perhaps have a few half ones in a cosy hostelry, or do whatever else might want doing on this his monthly visit to the town.

But no money would yet change hands. The tangler had sealed the deal with a spit on the palm of his hand and a handshake with the farmer. With this the farmer was precluded from selling to anyone else, regardless of what offer he might get. It could be a harsh enough constraint at times, but, as they say, *'dem was de rules!'*

The tangler's task was now to find another farmer to buy the said animal or animals for a price which would give him a tidy profit. It was only then that the first farmer would get his money.

And it was not only the farmers and tanglers that would come. Farmers wives would be hoping their husbands would fetch a good price for their animals and give a little to them to buy a new hat, or clothes for the kids at home who were growing up all too fast. The farmers themselves might head to the ironmongers for any bits and pieces they might need to keep the farm in good stead. Or to the drapery to get measured for a new Sunday suit.

All the traders in town were guaranteed to have the best day of the month. And especially the publicans, who would provide a

17

warm and friendly environment where farmers and tanglers could do their dealing over a few drinks while the women might sip a glass of claret in the snug.

The traders were mindful of the damage these animals packed into the streets could do to the windows and doors of their premises. The evening before the Fair Day, they would put out the *fair gates* to protect their premises. These were wooden railings which hooked together, stood perhaps two feet out from the front of the shop, with a hinged gate opposite the shop entrance. The animals could press up against these railings to their heart's content, the shopfronts were protected. For the rest of the month the railings would be stored in some shed or back yard.

III

Back to the reported invasion plan. When exactly was it supposed to happen? Tony, in his telling, never mentioned a date. The archives of the local newspaper, the Nationalist, might, I thought, provide that information.

I began my search in January 1940, concentrating on the editions on or just after the first Wednesday of each month. Everything was going along nicely as I saw Fair Day reports month after month. That the reports were published on the same day, a Wednesday, was due to the early start of the Fair: the news reporter could file his report well before mid-day while the paper wouldn't be printed until later that evening. For example:

> Wednesday 1st May: *Small fair, mostly composed of two year old bullocks and heifers. Mostly everything sold; late rates maintained. Not many strong cattle on offer, which sold readily at slightly better prices. Practically no beef, which met a slow demand.*

Wednesday 5th June: *Small fair; mostly everything sold. Strong cattle sold a little more readily. Anything nice made a fair price and everything cleared.*

But for July I could find no report. Did Fair Days stop during the war years, or was July just an anomaly? I kept going.

Wednesday 7th August: *Medium sized fair. Owing to drought business very dragging. Lot of cattle unsold. Beef sold readily at recent rates.*

Saturday 7th September: *Medium sized fair; good cattle scarce, for which there was good enquiry. Suitable stores for winter feeding sold easier. Thin cattle hard to dispose of, a fair clearance was however effected.*

July alone had no report. Could this be when news of the invasion arrived? I decided to look at the July 10th edition to see if perchance there was a late report. There wasn't. But I spotted this:

ÉIRE'S ATTACK DANGER :

The next great battle of the war may be fought on Éire territory, stated Mr. Seun Lemass.

Speaking of the possibilities of invasion or isolation, he said: "It is my duty to tell you that it is the considered opinion of the Government this country is facing one or both of these contingencies.

"I again stress the urgency of this matter. The dangers we foresee are not in this year or the year after, but possibly in this week or next week"

Some hours before the Minister spoke it was announced that mines are being placed off the Irish coast by the Government. Shipping will be notified.

All this seemed to confirm 3rd of July 1940 as the date of the anticipated invasion. Séan Lemass was a Government Minister and his speech certainly indicates that the Government had some intelligence warning of an imminent invasion around that time. Whether the Germans actually did plan to invade that day or whether someone in some Government Department in Dublin misread intelligence is a moot point at this stage, but we can have some confidence that the invasion warning Tony spoke of was issued in respect of that day.

IV

This sensitive and highly confidential information was passed on to the members of the Local Security Force in Clonmel on the evening of Tuesday 2nd of July, short enough notice you might think, but no doubt it was the soonest possible in the circumstances.

There was consternation. Tomorrow would be the Fair Day, when farmers for miles around would be up at the crack of dawn, or earlier, to drive their animals to market. And many would be accompanied by their good lady wives, who looked forward to this monthly excursion to town.

There were also, as we saw, the shops and pubs in Clonmel to consider. They would be looking forward to the best day trading of the month. And they would already have put up the fair gates.

Such were the matters to be discussed by the good men of the Local Security Force – and they were all men, not a woman among them: back then, everyone *knew* this was a job for men only. What should they do? They spent some considerable time discussing this grave matter. At the end of it all they decided that, regardless of the consequences, they had no option but to cancel the Fair Day.

Imagine if the Germans did indeed land and were advancing along the road from Dungarvan to Clonmel and there were farmers driving their cattle to market, it would be a disaster. You might say that having the road full of animals would be the best thing that could happen, as they would surely slow down the invasion. Maybe so. But then again, maybe not. The invaders might decide to shoot, or worse still, bomb the farmers and their animals if they didn't move quickly enough. No, that could not be allowed to happen.

The owners of shops and pubs in Clonmel could be contacted easily enough since they mostly lived over the premises. On hearing the news they were not happy, but on reflection they saw there was no alternative. The Fair Day of July 1940 would not happen and they would have to live with the consequences.

However getting word out to the farmers was another matter. The LSF would have to send a small detachment out along each of the roads leading into town to intercept the farmers and turn them back. The farmers would not be happy, but it had to be done.

The men went home for a few hours' sleep before heading out at the crack of dawn, at five o'clock in the morning in this summer month of July, out along the many roads that led to town. It had to be that ungodly hour for the farmers were known early risers, and they couldn't be let get too far from home before being turned back.

And so it was that at the village of Kilmanahan on the road between Clonmel to Dungarvan, Tony was meeting farmers and telling them to go home. For the most part, when they heard the reason why, they grumbled about the inconvenience, cursed Hitler and reluctantly turned for home.

One farmer was incensed by the Germans' lack of consideration, and his highly indignant response summed up exactly and succinctly what everyone in Clonmel and all the other farmers were thinking:

> *"Jesus Christ and in the name of all that's holy, couldn't the Germans pick any day other than the Fair Day in Clonmel to invade?*

Quite so.

V

Later that morning, having completed their civic duty, Ned, a local publican and a member of the LSF out on duty that morning, decided that such a civic minded group performing this important duty, couldn't be allowed to go home without a small celebration and he invited them to join him for a few drinks in his public house on Gladstone Street. A fitting end to a job well done.

Fortunately, the Germans never did appear that day. Or indeed any other day during the Emergency.

The Strange Case of Timmy O'Neill

I

Bay Lough, an old corrie lake in the Knockmealdown Mountains, together with the legends surrounding it are central to the story of Timmy O'Neill.

But before telling you about Timmy O'Neill, let me first cast my mind back to the 50s, when often on a Sunday afternoon my parents, grandmother, brother and sisters would all pile into Da's jalopy and off we would go for a drive, or a *drassen* as he would say.

Sometimes our *drassen* would take us to the village of Clogheen and from there up the winding road leading South until at the last hairpin bend we would be at the Vee. Looking north on a clear day we could see all the way to the Slieve Bloom mountains. We youngsters used to compete to see which of us would be the first to pick out the Devil's Bit, a gap in that mountain ridge. Legend has it that one day while the devil was traversing Ireland he stopped at the Slieve Blooms, took a bite out of it and spat it out. Where it landed became the famous rock of Cashel.

Look south and you will see the Sugarloaf peak while to the west lies Bay Lough and beyond that, the Knockshanahullion peak. I remember being told that Bay Lough is a bottomless lake, and that if you tried to swim across, somewhere in the middle you were likely to be sucked down, never to be seen again. I never did try, mostly because the water is always bloody cold. The lake, being in the shadow of the hills, is rarely exposed to the warming rays of the sun.

Curiosity about the legends surrounding Bay Lough led me in later life to develop a keen interest in myths and legends. In all my research I have been unable to find any written reference to the warning about being pulled under Bay Lough. This remains for me firmly in the realm of oral myth or tradition.

But there is another legend relating to Bay Lough, which may or may not be related to the risk of being dragged under, that is the one about of Petticoat Loose. There are quite a few stories about Petticoat Loose, most of which relate back to the 18th or 19th century. But the one which I believe to be the authentic story goes back much further, back to the 14th Century. This story is told by Rose Springfield in *The Legend of the Seven Bishops*[1]. The following is the relevant excerpt:

> *There was once a holy man. He was riding through the wild places of Ireland, teaching the people holy things. As he rode at the back of Slievenamon, he was coming close to Drangan, when he met a very wicked woman carrying a basket.*
>
> *"What have you in the basket?" he asked.*
>
> *"I have seven puppy dogs," said the wicked woman.*
>
> *Now the holy man knew she was Petticoat Loose, a very wicked woman, for nothing was hid from him because he was so holy. "Open your basket!" says he to her.*
>
> *"I will not," says she, as cocky as the nose of a drawing room bellows.*
>
> *"Open it at once!" says he, making the Sign of the Cross at her. So she opened it and there were seven baby boys, all alive.*
>
> *"Give me the babies," says he to her, "and I will bring them up to be holy men."*
>
> *Well, she struggled against his will, but he pointed his fingers at her, and said he "would put horns on her so that*

---

[1] Recorded in the book *'Romantic Slievenamon in History, Folklore and Song: A Tipperary Anthology'*, edited by James Maher and published in 1954; also available on the Kilkenny Archæological Society website.

then she would turn into a puck goat". So she gave up the babies and the basket and all, and he mounted his horse to ride away. But before he went he said:

"O wicked woman, I will give you another chance for your soul. Go to Bay Lough by the old road across the Knockmealdowns to the river Blackwater, and stay there and repent your sins!"

But Petticoat Loose did not care for God or holy men so she had to stay at Bay Lough and could not get away. Still, she kept on being wicked, and had an enormous son who lived in Bay Lough, and was so big 'he could eat a bullock in one meal'; and when he spit the spit was so big that the lake would almost overflow, and his spit was so bitter that no dog, or cow, or heifer, or bullock will ever drink the water no matter what drought there is on them.

And Petticoat Loose went on growing more and more wicked. Although as thin as a lath, yet when she sat on a cart she was so heavy that any horse or ass would break into a lather of sweat and would be unable to move the cart while she was on it.

And the holy man heard of this, even in France, and he sent back word that she had lost that chance and now she must go to the Red Sea and remain there until she drained it with a tailor's thimble.

I wondered where the Red Sea reference came from. Some years ago, while in Reykjavik at a conference on the Icelandic Sagas, I met and developed a friendship with Khalid Ibn Ahmed Al Halabi from the Library of Alexendria where he is the curator of *The Repository of Folklore, Myths & Legends*. I wrote asking if he had any knowledge or could find any record of an Irish witch, Petticoat Loose, being banished to the Red Sea. Three months later I received a reply:

Library of Alexandria
28 Shalawal 1428[1]

My Dear Irish Friend.

As always, it was such a delight to hear from you.

I searched here in Alexandria and could find no reference to your Irish Petticoat Loose. I then took it upon myself to write to some colleagues in other National Archives which are adjacent to the Red Sea, namely Cairo, Amman, Jerusalem, Addis Ababa, Sana'a and Jeddah.

Replies took some time but I'm afraid I must disappoint you. Neither I nor any of my colleagues could find any reference to your Irish witch anywhere in these parts.

I trust you are keeping well and hope to see you at the Heraklion conference next year.

Ever in friendship,

Khalid

The Red Sea reference remains a mystery to me. I suspect it may have been added much later to reassure people that they had nothing to fear from Bay Lough. And perhaps the legend about being pulled under was spread about to discourage anyone putting themselves at risk of encountering Petticoat Loose?

II

Timothy O'Neill was an only child. He lived in Clogheen with his father Mícheál Óg, or Young Michael, Óg having been added to his name to distinguish him from his father, also called Mícheál. Sadly, his mother, Sheila, had died giving birth to

---

[1] Islamic calendar, or 8th November 2007 in the Western calendar

him, so there was just Timmy and his Dad. It was a happy home and Timmy grew up to be a responsible if occasionally somewhat mischievous teenager, at times prone to little acts of bravado. One day, when he was sixteen years old, he told his Dad he was thinking of swimming across Bay Lough. His Dad reminded him of the legend of swimmers disappearing in the middle of the lake.

"You don't really believe that old *piseog*[1], now do you, Dad?" he asked. His Dad did not immediately reply, but instead reached up to the top shelf of books and took down one, *'Romantic Slievenamon'*.

"Dad, you read all those stories to me years ago, but they're just folklore tales. You don't seriously expect me to decide whether to swim across Bay Lough based on some old legend?" Timmy responded. "I remember the story of Petticoat Loose and Bay Lough and it says nothing about being dragged down if you try to swim across. Anyway, didn't some Bishop banish her to the Red Sea forever? If there's any truth in the legend, it's the people out in that part of the world that should be worried about her. But I'm sure they never heard of her."

"Your memory serves you well," replied Mícheál Óg, "still, it's no harm to be mindful of old tales. They often come with a grain of truth. But you're old enough and responsible enough to make up your own mind. Just be careful."

A few days later, Timmy was out with his friends John-Joe Moran and Fergie McCarthy. He told them of his plan to swim across the lake. John-Joe responded at once: "I wouldn't swim in that lake if you paid me. I'm not going to risk the wrath of that Petticoat Loose one." Fergie added: "And besides the water is always bloody freezing. You won't catch me swimming there."

"God, aren't ye two fraidy cats," said Timmy, "do ye seriously

---

[1] Piseog: Superstition

believe those Old Wives Tales? Anyhow, will ye at least come with me, if only to be a witness to this heroic event? And of course to go off crying wolf if the dreaded witch Petticoat Loose decides to turn up." The two lads said they would.

Next day, warm and sunny, the three friends cycled up to the Vee and Bay Lough. Timmy dipped his toes in the water. "You were right, Fergie. Bloody freezing," he said before diving in. He swam around near the shore for a few minutes before shouting to the others, "I only want to swim over, not back again, so will you lads walk around to the other side with my towel and clothes?" "Yeah, sure," shouted John-Joe.

Bay Lough is about 200m across, or something over 300m to walk around from one side to the other. As Timmy swam, the two friends dawdled along, blatherering away, and occasionally looking over the lake to be sure their friend was OK. They were about half way around when John-Joe heard a piercing scream. He immediately looked across the lake, and to his horror there was Timmy struggling in the water, waving his hands and screaming for help. Fergie had also heard the scream.

The two lads, without saying a word, immediately striped off to swim out to help him. But Timmy just disappeared before their very eyes, vanished without trace. They dived and swam under water looking for him, but he was nowhere to be seen.

At first they thought Timmy was playing some prank and that he would suddenly appear from nowhere. But as the minutes passed it became ever more apparent this was not going to happen. What could have happened? Could he really have been taken under? They were terrified. How could they explain to Mícheál Óg what had happened?

Stranger still, Fergie found Timmy's togs on the shore while his clothes, which he had been carrying, were missing. The lads were in bits. They dreaded the very thought of going back to Clogheen.

III

Pranks however were the furthest things from Timmy's mind at that moment. He was in a panic. Something was holding his leg and pulling him down. At first he struggled, but it was no use. He found himself being pulled deeper and deeper underwater.

He was in turmoil. His mind was racing. Could this legend of Petticoat Loose and Bay Lough really be true? And if it was, why would she be here in Bay Lough and not out in the Red Sea? That's surely where she should be. Wasn't it?

Or was there something else altogether responsible for this? Whether Petticoat Loose was or wasn't in the Red Sea, there was still that legend of being pulled under if you tried to swim across. Was this legend true? And if so, who or what would be pulling him down?

All these thoughts were swirling around inside and he thought his head was about to burst. Why, oh why didn't he take heed of his Dad's warning? He tried struggling but it was no use. He was being held with an iron grip. He just couldn't break free. But the strange thing was he didn't seem to be struggling for air.

Several seconds later, and while all this turmoil was still racing through his mind, he was pulled into what seemed like a short underwater tunnel. At the end of the tunnel he emerged into another world, full of light. He found himself on a rocky beach, with a beautiful young woman beside him.

Timmy was bewildered. He did not know what to make of all this. At least, he thought to himself, I seem to have been taken by a beautiful woman, not an ugly old hag. At least it's not Petticoat Loose, he thought.

"Where am I?" he asked, "and who are you?"

Not in his wildest dream could he have anticipated the reply to that: "I am Niamh and Céad Míle Fáilte[1] to Tír nÓg[2]!"

He was stunned. Tír na nÓg beneath Bay Lough? Surely impossible!

"But this is ridiculous," he said. "Everyone around here knows the legend of Bay Lough, but it says nothing about Tír na nÓg. It's all about that evil witch, that ugly old hag Petticoat Loose. Anyway, she was banished to the Red Sea. But you're not an ugly old hag. And Tír na nÓg is just another old legend. I don't believe in those old *piseogs*."

"Not believing is of little consequence now that you're actually here," came the reply. "You just managed to stumble on one of the portals to Tír na nÓg, on a day when it is active. You could swim across Bay Lough another time and nothing would happen. But not today, as you have just discovered. Tales like Petticoat Loose have a habit of twisting the true story over time. And there are many stories about her. That there are so many is a sure sign that the truth about her, whoever she was, indeed if she ever was, has long since been lost. The one truth is the one which doesn't feature in the legend of Petticoat Loose: if you try to swim across Bay Lough you may be dragged down."

Timmy was somewhat reassured by this, although this story of Tír na nÓg under Bay Lough was not so easy to accept. "But where is this 'here'?" Timmy asked.

"Let's take a walk," she said as she stretched out her hand to Timmy. He took it and she guided him through some rather large rocks. Soon, what had seemed like a small place opened up to a vast world. Sunshine, blue skies, woodland, shimmering sea, and seemingly endless meadow lands stretching off as far as the eye

---

[1] Céad Míle Fáilte - One hundred thousand welcomes
[2] Tír na nÓg – Land of Eternal Youth

could see. Where he wondered was the Sugarloaf? Knockmealdown mountain? The Vee? Clogheen? It was all too much to take in.

"How long have you been here?" he asked.

"Oh, about 700 years now, I think. It can be hard to keep track", she replied. "Such is life in Tír na nÓg."

"We learned about Oisín and Tír na nÓg in school. But nobody believed it was a real place. Anyway, nobody could live to be 700 years old."

"Whether you believe or not makes no difference to the facts," she replied. "But first things first. You must meet our King Manannán. He always wants to meet new people."

"King?" Timmy said. "We fought long and hard in this country to rid ourselves of Kings and Queens and I'm not at all sure I want to go bowing and scraping in front of a King."

"You should have paid more attention to your history. We had Kings and Queens in this country long before those from across the water imposed themselves on us. Surely you remember Medb and Brian Boru among many others?"

Timmy felt a little chastened. "OK, take me to this King Manannán. Don't ever remember hearing about him before. How should I address him? Will I have to bow or kneel in his presence?"

"Relax," said Niamh, "just show respect as you would in the presence of any new person you meet. And take your hands out of your pockets."

Timmy looked down. This is strange he thought as he noticed that he did indeed have his hands in his pockets. But more to the point, where were his swimming togs? How come he was now in his shorts and T-shirt, which he had left with John-Joe and Fergie? How did that happen? Curiouser and curiouser it was getting down here.

So off he went to meet the King. Somewhere in the back of his mind the name Manannán rang a bell. Wasn't Manannán Mac Lir the King of Tír na nÓg? The first thing he noted was there was no crown and no throne. That at least made him more at ease. Manannán was relaxing, a big hulk of a man, naked except for a loin cloth, stretched out on a pile of cushions, drinking a cup of tea, or at least Timmy presumed it was tea.

The King looked up when he saw Timmy. "Now young man, who are you and what brings you down here?"

Timmy, head down, hands out of his pockets, mumbled: "Timmy O'Neill from Clogheen. Don't know why I'm here, it just happened when I was swimming in Bay Lough."

The King leant forward, hand cupped behind his ear. "Speak up young man, I can't make out what you're mumbling."

Now Timmy all but shouted: "I don't know, it just happened when I was swimming in Bay Lough. Niamh caught my leg and pulled me down and suddenly I was in another world. And somewhere along the way I lost my swimming togs and somehow got into my clothes. I have no idea how. Niamh tells me I'm in Tír na nÓg, the land of eternal youth. Rather strange and hard to come to terms with since I never believed any of those legends. But in reality, all I want to do is go back home to my Dad."

"I see, I see," said the King. "Young Niamh here has a habit of doing that occasionally, pulling people down from the middle of Bay Lough. She's my daughter, you know. Of course everyone from Clogheen to Lismore and for miles and miles around knows better than to swim across Bay Lough for fear of Petticoat Loose, even though that same legend says the old witch was banished to the Red Sea. A bit of a contradiction there it seems. And you can rest assured she is not here."

Timmy replied: "Any warning I ever heard was about Petticoat Loose. I never heard that Bay Lough had anything to do with Tír na nÓg. And I'm just remembering, would you be Manannán Mac Lir, by any chance?"

"So you did learn something, it seems. You can just use my name, Manannán, or as most do, just call me Manann for short."

"Yes, Manannán. Thank you Manannán. I mean Manann," Timmy replied awkwardly.

"Hmmm," said the King. "I'm afraid you'll have to loosen up young man. Relax. I'm sure you're wondering what happens next, how long you can or will have to stay here, what your father and friends will be thinking."

That's exactly what Timmy was thinking before the King continued. But he wondered what this 'how long you can or *will have to* stay' was all about? Could he not just decide whether he did or didn't want to stay in Tír na nÓg? He might have expected something like that from Petticoat Loose, but surely not from the King of the wondrous Tír na nÓg? However, he said nothing.

Manannán continued: "Well, you say all you want to do is go home. But in the first instance, you and everyone from Clogheen to Lismore and beyond knows of the risk in swimming across Bay Lough, so you can hardly complain about finding yourself here. Now the practicalities. When you were in the middle of the lake and Niamh grabbed you by the ankle, and you started to struggle, your friends saw this and immediately started to swim out to rescue you. But what happened next may surprise you. At the very moment you were dragged under, time froze in the world above, and will stay frozen for up to three days. So you are not missing, no one is looking for you, you are just caught in a time warp, so to speak.

"'Why three days?' no doubt you are thinking. Well everything down here is in threes. So you can stay here three days, three months, years, decades, centuries. You can only leave on one of those anniversaries of your arrival.

"Staying for three days will give you time to experience the wonderous life down here. When you return, your friends will have no concept or understanding that you were missing at all. But there is a downside. Your problem will be that you will never be able to talk about down here without raised eyebrows looking back at you and being exposed to ridicule. Or perhaps worse. But you'll probably be able to talk about it as if it were some dream you had. An interesting story to tell your friends.

"Any time after three days that you decide to return you will have been missing and a big search party will have spent days or weeks looking for you. In the absence of any sign of you or your body, they will presume you are dead.

"What then will they think when you calmly arrive back in Clogheen alive and well in three months or in three years? They will demand an explanation. What will you tell them? How will you explain your absence? When you try to tell them you were in Tír na nÓg, what will they think? Do you think they will believe you?

"Three decades might be easier. Your father may or may not be still alive. Your friends for the most part will have departed Clogheen for other places. It could be a lonely return.

"But then you could simply decide to stay here and enjoy the life of eternal youth. Down here, you will always be the age you were when you arrived. Whenever you do decide to leave, if you ever do, you will immediately age by the length of time you are here. If you stay for three decades, thirty years, you will immediately age to 46 years old. Oisín, you may recall, stayed for three centuries. You would at most be a legend by that time, unknown to any living person, and probably forgotten. Then as soon as you touch the ground you will immediately become a 316 years old man and die. Oisín went on horseback, with strict instructions not to dismount if he wanted to return to Tír na nÓg. But he couldn't resist the urge to touch and kiss the soil of Erin he had missed for so long. The rest, as they say, is history.

"And then again, maybe three days would suit you – you would return without being missed, and who knows? you might even persuade your Dad to return with you? That way you wouldn't be carrying around the story of Tír na Óg, afraid to tell anyone for fear of ridicule. Now that might be a neat solution.

"So now, young Timmy, the choice is yours. The first deadline will be 72 hours after your arrival. If you want to leave then, you must come tomorrow evening. Like Cinderella, before the last stroke of midnight. Three days is the longest you can stay here without being missed in Clogheen. You will have time to experience our world. But of course that will also give you time to think of the delights of staying here and to hell with the consequences, as they say. Your decision, young Timmy."

Timmy replied: "There's no need for me to wait until tomorrow evening, Manann. I can tell you now that I will go back after three days. I really would like to get back home to my Dad and friends before I'm missed."

Manannán's reply was not quite what Timmy expected: "That's all very well young Timmy, but experience has told me that those who make an instant decision not to stay without knowing anything of the delights of Tír na nÓg, all too frequently regret it. So now, we make sure the new visitor is properly informed before deciding to leave. If you still feel tomorrow evening that you want to leave before you're missed, come back here before midnight."

With that, and before he had a chance to say anything more, Niamh took him by the hand and led him away on a brief tour. "You can wander around at your leisure. Talk to anyone you meet. They're all very friendly and they'll be delighted to meet a newcomer with all the latest news and gossip from above. If you fancy a bite to eat, there'll be lots of people cooking barbecues or just having a snack. Anyone can join in and partake of what's going. And if you fancy a swim with no risk of being pulled under, just strip off and dive into the sea. Nobody wears swim suits and nobody is self-conscious or embarrassed when it comes to naked bodies. I'll leave you to make your own way, but don't forget about tomorrow night's deadline if you want to avoid being missed."

On reflection, Timmy felt these arrangements were OK. He could sample the delights of Tír na nÓg for three days before anyone missed him. But also he was in no doubt that he would return before he was missed.

Timmy looked around at this enchanting place. While waiting for the three day deadline, he wanted to make the most of his time in the magical Tír na nÓg.

He decided to go for a swim before eating. The sea was pleasantly warm in stark contrast to the freezing waters of Bay Lough. He could live with this, he thought.

Afterwards he joined a group cooking a barbecue. The food was delicious. Everyone wanted to meet the new member of the community. They had all sorts of questions about the world above. Strange, he thought, was the most important topic of conversation: Football and Hurling. How was this club or that county doing? Who won last years All Ireland? Rugby and soccer too. Six Nations Championship, European Club Championships, English Premier League and the World Cup. Most of the people seemed to have been around so long that it was a wonder how they even knew of such things.

That night he slept under the stars. What a magnificent sky! There was no moon and he could see the Milky Way in all its magnificence stretched across the sky. It was a sight to behold. It took him ages to nod off.

Next morning he was offered the chance to go horse riding across the meadows. He had never been up on a horse, but a very pretty young girl, Deirdre, gave him a quick introduction and led him off at a canter. They spent hours riding around, taking in the magnificent sights, stopping for a picnic lunch and a swim in a cool stream. He became very attracted to his beautiful companion.

He was back in time for another barbecue. Here he was, having tasted some of the delights of Tír na nÓg, but he would soon be going home. He wanted to be back before he was missed. The delights, enchanting as they were, were not enough to convince him to stay.

Deirdre appeared again at the barbecue and he became engrossed in conversation with her. He would miss her, but he would not let that sway him. The deadline was almost upon him before he realised it. He made his excuses, saying he just had to go or he'd miss his chance to go back home. He rushed off towards Manannán's cave.

IV

But Timmy didn't leave the next day. On his way to Manannán he ran into Niamh, who started to ask him how much he had enjoyed his time there. Out of politeness he delayed several moments before telling her he HAD to go or he'd miss the deadline. But then he heard the last of the twelve peals of midnight just before he got to Manannán's cave.

"Hello, young Timmy. Since you didn't come to me by midnight, I presume you intend to stay with us for a few months at least."

"But it's only just midnight," Timmy said. "I really do want to leave before the three days are up. I was totally absorbed in the wonderful experience of Tír na nÓg, and then I ran to be on time. But on the way I bumped into Niamh which it seems delayed me vital seconds before the last stroke of midnight. But surely a couple of seconds doesn't count? And only seconds short of 24 hours before I will be missed? You knew yesterday that I wanted to leave before I was missed. Can I leave tomorrow? Please, pretty please?"

Manannán raised his eyebrows. Doesn't look too good, thought Timmy, and it wasn't.

"Timmy, this as you say is a wondrous place. We have very few rules and I explained to you the rule of three for leaving. I also made clear the deadline for deciding to return without being missed. You missed that deadline. Whether by a second or a few hours, a deadline is a deadline. You were your own man when you decided to swim across Bay Lough, you were aware of the risks, but you went ahead. You had the option of leaving without being missed, but you let the deadline pass. I thought you would take that option to be able to bring your Dad back with you, but apparently not. The next option will be in two months and twenty-eight days. Let me know by midnight five days before that if you want to leave then."

"What about three weeks? What's the deadline for going back after three weeks?" he asked.

"I'm sorry Timmy, but I never mentioned a three week deadline. The next option is three months," Manannán replied.

That was it. There was no more Timmy could do about it. He was trapped down there. Yet, if it was such a wondrous place, and if Niamh and Manannán were such wonderful people, why would they deny him the right to leave? Why were they holding him against his wishes? And did Niamh deliberately delay him for those vital seconds so that he arrived late for this artificial deadline? Fully 24 hours before he would be missed? *Whether by a second or a few hours, a deadline is a deadline* Manannán had said. Why such strict rules in this wonderland? Such a web of contradictions.

Maybe if he could find that tunnel where he came in, might he be able to escape back up to the lake on his own? Worth a try, he thought, as he wandered around trying to find that place. But try as he might, it was nowhere to be seen. He felt more and more trapped with every minute.

For a while he tried to rationalise the situation. After all, a place like Tír na nÓg couldn't just have people coming and going all the time. Maybe the rules were reasonable. But he never did quite convince himself.

He had no option but to remain on, but it was no longer wondrous. Yes, he enjoyed it some of the time, but this enjoyment was tainted with the knowledge that he was being held against his wishes. Maybe rules are rules, but what sort of a person would be so rigid as to forbid him the possibility of getting back to his Dad before he was missed, all because he was a few stupid seconds late for a stupid artificial deadline a full day before he would be able to leave? Had Manannán given no consideration to how his Dad might be feeling? This was all wrong.

His thoughts turned to John-Joe and Fergie who would be at a loss to understand what had happened, and unable to explain how he had disappeared. John-Joe would notice that somehow Timmy's clothes, which he had been carrying around the lake, had inexplicably disappeared. He would now be a missing person and they would be talking to Timmy's Dad, making statements to the Guards and taking part in search parties, combing the place for miles around: lake, mountains, woodland. But they would find nothing. Except his bicycle which he had left at the side of the lake.

And worst of all, his Dad would be distraught and inconsolable. Timmy and his Dad were so close.

No doubt the Garda sub-aqua squad would be called in. They would search the lake, but would find nothing. They would wonder how a body could sink and stay down.

Would Niamh be watching out and catch one of the divers by the leg and pull him down? He didn't think so. As they would be kitted out with SCUBA equipment, and there would probably be more than one, he suspected she would not want to be spotted by a second diver while taking hold of one. And anyway, Manannán had said the Bay Lough portal only opens occasionally. No! Better leave behind a mystery of just the one person missing, he supposed.

There was no three week deadline in this 'rule of three'. Why? he wondered. But in a strange way Timmy was thankful for that. After three weeks, in all probability search parties would still be out looking for him. How could he just bump into one and explain what had happened? How could he wander back nonchalantly, in perfect health, not a blemish on his body, and explain where he had been? No, he couldn't face that. Three months would not be so bad, he thought. With the strong likelihood that search parties would no longer be out looking for him, he could slip quietly in home to his Dad before anyone knew.

When he finally did get back, what would he say to his Dad? What would he write in his statement to the Guards? That he had just popped down to Tír na nÓg for a while and was back now? Would they just laugh at him and have a good laugh between themselves, before calling in the psychiatrist? He could see himself being sent to the mental hospital for a very long time.

But there was no question of staying beyond three months. His Dad would already have suffered untold anxiety. This time there would be no missed deadline.

Despite the wonderful life he experienced when he first arrived - swimming in the warm tropical-like waters, joining in barbecues, horse-riding with Deirdre - there appeared to be a distinct absence of happiness and enthusiasm for life among the people he met. Definitely not what he would expect in the magical and wonderous Tír na nÓg of legends. Very strange, he thought.

He had made a point of meeting and talking to people about their life in Tír na nÓg, and whether they ever thought of leaving. But strangely enough as far as he could figure out, no one seemed to have had any thoughts about the people or the communities where they had lived. How had they got here? Were they happy in this underworld? Did they ever think of going back? But try as he might, they wouldn't say, just gave vague answers which really told him nothing. They didn't seem interested in anything.

Why were they not enjoying this wondrous Tír na nÓg? Why were they still here? All lonely, isolated people?

And even stranger, he never seemed to meet the same people twice. Where were they?

Had all those people got here by swimming across Bay Lough? A lot of them didn't look like the type who would just decide to dive into the lake. But how else would they get here? Niamh had referred to portals, so he presumed there must be others. But where? However the people he met got to be there, they were not revealing it. For all the talking, he was none the wiser.

Time and again his mind drifted back to that uneasy feeling that everything down here was not as it seemed. It struck him that in his mind he sometimes described where he was as an underworld. Other people he met had also used that term. Yes, that was an accurate enough description given that he did get there by going down under Bay Lough. But there was of course also The Underworld of legends. Could it be that he was in The Underworld? Were all these people trapped down here? Was there in fact some evil dimension to all this? Was Niamh really who she seemed to be? Or could it be that behind a guise, she was in fact that ugly hag, that witch of legends, Petticoat Loose? And if so, who then was playing at Manannán Mac Lir? Petticoat Loose's son? "No," he thought, "this is only my mind playing games." Although the Tír na nÓg narrative just didn't ring true, if Manannán and Niamh were not who they said they were, they never let down their guard. Except for one strange incident some half way through his stay.

He spotted the two of them and it seemed for a fraction of a second as if Niamh was an old hag, and Manannán a young thug. But that same instant this very unsavoury appearance disappeared.

He thought back to the story in that book, Romantic Slievenamon. Petticoat Loose had an enormous son, so big that, as he remembered, *"he could eat a bullock at one meal"*. And Petticoat Loose was described as being *"as thin as a lath"*. Perhaps by some sorcery or black magic they were able to present themselves as the mythical Manannán and Niamh of Tír na nÓg legend while being in reality the old hag and her thuggish son? Could that be so? Could it be that they were in league with the Devil himself?

He couldn't be sure of what he really saw. Maybe it was just himself imagining his worst fears, that he was being held captive in some twilight zone, some underworld that seemed at the same time both enchanting and threatening. Whatever it was, he was more and more determined by the day to leave at the three month deadline.

But there was one chink in his armour. His riding companion and object of his romantic desires, Deirdre. After the three day deadline passed, she asked if he'd accompany her on another canter across the meadows. She had really enjoyed their first day together. Of course he said yes. They spent endless days riding out over meadows and through forests, stopping for picnics and swimming lazily in streams or sea. And even better, she seemed to be returning his romantic overtures.

As the three month deadline approached, he became conflicted. He was in love. Deirdre and himself were blossoming together and the thought of leaving her was causing him more and more distress. But behind it all he remained focused on going back. He told Deirdre that he just had to see his Dad again, surely she could understand this. Of course she could, she replied, but started to sob saying how much she would miss him. She begged him to promise he would come back, hugging and kissing him. Timmy knew he couldn't make that promise so he just said he would very much like to see her again, but first he must go to Clogheen. He headed once more to Manannán's cave, this time comfortably ahead of the deadline.

"So you're ready to leave, young Timmy? I must say I'm somewhat surprised. I hear you and Deirdre are having a bit of a romance and thought she might have enticed you to stay. But this time you have met the deadline so it's your own decision. Do you know what you will do when you get back? How will you explain your absence in Clogheen?"

"I don't know, it's going to be quite a problem. I'll just have to find a way to deal with it." Timmy replied quietly.

"I have no doubt you will, young Timmy," Manannán replied. "It's been a pleasure having you with us and I'm sure you will be missed by everyone, and by none more than Deirdre. Niamh will look for you next Wednesday morning to bring you to the surface of Bay Lough. After that you will be on your own.

"Until the next time", he continued. "For I have no doubt you will return to us some day soon. Perhaps you will want to see Deirdre again? Maybe your Dad will come too? Now that would be a neat way for both of you to avoid the potentially ugly consequences of trying to explain your absence."

Timmy kept his counsel and said nothing apart from a polite "Good-bye, Manannán".

Early the next Wednesday morning, Niamh took Timmy back to the rock formation where he had first entered with her. Funnily enough it was just about where he had thought it should be, even though when he looked for it some weeks ago, he couldn't find it. "Now, why was that?" he thought to himself. "To ensure I couldn't escape?"

Yet Niamh was very friendly and seemed supportive of his leaving, saying that she had no doubt it would be a great and joyful occasion for him seeing his Dad again, before continuing: "You must hold my hand while we swim into the tunnel and up through the cold waters of Bay Lough. As soon as I let go you will immediately want to surface for air. You will be back where you started your journey here, only three months older. Swim to the western side of the lake, where you were headed three months ago, and there amid the Rhododendrons you will find some clothes, and some food. You will never see me again."

"Unless," she added with a glint in her eye, "unless you decide to swim across Bay Lough again. Perhaps having regaled your father with the joys and wonders of life here in Tír na nÓg, you will both want to come here – to avoid all the problems with your disappearance and your sudden and inexplicable reappearance. And did I hear something of a budding romance between you and Deirdre? Now surely you have good reason to return to us. Farewell." But Timmy didn't engage, he just said a polite goodbye. Niamh guided him into the water, through the tunnel and back to the surface of Bay Lough.

V

Timmy broke surface in the early hours of a cold October morning. He was shivering as he swam to the western shore. He got out of the water and searched among the Rhododendrons. Sure enough, there was a bag with some clothes, a fine breakfast roll which he wolfed down, and a sandwich which he would keep for later.

Interesting, he thought that Niamh could leave them beyond the shores of the lake. Surely Niamh of Tír na nÓg couldn't touch the soil of Erin without immediately aging and dying? Then he wondered whether Petticoat Loose could, if indeed that was who 'Niamh' really was. Or was there some sorcery involved? Once again he wondered whether Petticoat Loose might be in league with the Devil. But no matter. He had more important things to think about.

He rubbed his hand over his face and felt a wispy beard. Of course, he had started to shave several months ago, but now he hadn't shaved for three months, so the bit of a beard was unsurprising.

Foremost in his mind was going to meet his Dad. He knew he would have been devastated. But he would not go there just yet, he would go under cover of darkness to ensure it would be his Dad who first saw him. Also, he wanted to take some time to get his thoughts in order and savour his new freedom.

He looked around and felt so pleased to be back in his own familiar world. It was a cold morning and he was shivering when he emerged from the water; then he stumbled and fell, cutting his knee – all things that could never have happened where he had just come from. But he felt free and alive for the first time in three months.

He decided to take a chance and climb Knockshanahullion to help while away the hours before he would return home under cover of darkness. As not so many climbed there, he thought it unlikely he would come across anyone who might recognise him. If he did spot someone, he would just keep the head down and keep going. As it happened, there was no one else up there that day.

As he walked, he kept going over and over the experience of the past three months. Suddenly something came to him. He remembered how Mannanán had said Oisín had been three hundred years in Tír na nÓg before returning to Erin. That was a fatal mistake. Now it came to him. In the story of Niamh and Oisín, Oisín returned to Ireland after three years in Tír na nÓg. But in Tír na nÓg time moved at a snail's pace such that one year there was the equivalent of one hundred years in our world. That is why he suddenly aged when he dismounted the horse to kiss the soil of Erin.

Timmy hadn't spotted that at the time. He had been down in that underworld for three months. If it had really been Tír na nÓg, he should now be one hundred times three months or twenty five years older. He should be forty-one, but he was still a 16 year old teenager. He had aged no more than the three months he was away.

A little while later he remembered that Petticoat Loose could in fact stray a short distance from the lake. How else could she in olden times have sat on the back of carts passing by? That would explain how 'Niamh' had been able to leave the bag of clothes in the Rhododendron bushes.

His mind drifted back to when he was first dragged under. When he had asked Niamh how long she had been there, she replied 700 years. Another fatal mistake which he should have spotted there and then, only he was too much in awe of everything that was happening. Oisín returned to Ireland at the time of St. Patrick, about 1,600 years ago. But if he remembered correctly the story of Petticoat Loose as recorded in 'Romantic Slievenamon', dated back to the 14th century. There was the 700 years!

Everything was falling into place. What he imagined he saw one day, that for one brief moment he had caught a glimpse of 'Niamh' and 'Manannán' appearing as Petticoat Loose and her son, was reality. He hadn't been in Tír na nÓg at all, rather he was in Petticoat Loose's underworld to which she was banished, and cute witch that she was, she was using her guile to trap others down there with her. And they nearly succeeded in trapping him too.

But if they really were Petticoat Loose and her son, why did they let him leave at all? While they had given him the option of returning without being missed, they made sure he missed the deadline.

After three months, both Petticoat Loose and her son carefully planted the suggestion that returning with his Dad to that wonderful place would be preferable to dealing with the consequences of his absence and his own inexplicable return.

Then there was Deirdre. Was she too part of the plot? Was she feigning romantic interest just to get him to stay? How come she was the only person he met more than once? Was her 'romance' all part of an elaborate scheme to get another captive for their underworld?

His thoughts turned back to the legend in Romantic Slievenamon. Petticoat Loose had been banished to Bay Lough by a very holy man, a Bishop, now long since dead. But whatever about the Red Sea dimension, he was now sure Petticoat Loose was still trapped in Bay Lough. She must still under his power, the power of holiness. Surely she would not have the freedom to trap any and all in her underworld, just like that. The more he thought about their tricks to get him to stay, the more he realised this was all about getting him to decide to stay. That way they would not be trapping him, rather he would be agreeing to join them. Would that be their way around the power of good and holiness?

He thought again of all those listless people he met in that underworld. Perhaps occasionally, a solitary, lonely person wandered down to the shores of Bay Lough and stood gazing at the water, hoping for some inspiration to ease their troubled mind? And at that moment a beguiling Niamh appeared presenting Tír na nÓg as the answer to their prayers? Did they then fall for some trap in which they found themselves agreeing to stay? And once they agreed there was no going back? He simply would not have met anyone who had escaped the clutches of Petticoat Loose.

Those 'other portals' were a lie. There were no other portals.

He was now sure that Deirdre was part of the plot. There was no other explanation for her being the only one to show interest in anything, but especially in him. All the others down there, whom he ever met only once, were so upset and embarrassed that they had been tricked, that they wouldn't talk about it.

Now, he thought, he understood everything. Whatever sliver of a chance there was of falling for Deirdre was now gone. His walk on

Knockshanahullion had done him the power of good.

He was down from the mountain by mid-afternoon. He hung back out of easy sight, ate his sandwich, and waited. A little later he saw a group of four men coming down towards the nearby Marian Shrine. They made for a car with a foreign registration. He noted the French accent, so he felt safe enough. He walked over and saluted them.

"Great day on the mountains," he said. "How far did ye go?"

"As far as Knockmealdown, then to Knockshane and down. A great day. Ireland is such a beautiful country. And you, where did you go?"

"Knockshanahullion," said Timmy replied. "It's over there," he said pointing towards the east. It's my favourite around here. Very few people seem to go there, can't figure out why."

They replied that they didn't know about that route. "Maybe tomorrow we come back. We are staying at Lismore." It felt good to have spoken to some real people, even if only for a few moments.

He continued to loiter around the area, taking care to remain discretely out of sight of any would-be passers-by who might recognise him. But all was quiet. It was dark before 8 o'clock on this cold October evening. He kept moving to keep himself warm. The moon rose and it was full. Using the moon's height in the sky as a guide, he waited until he felt it must be near midnight. He followed the old road to Clogheen where there would be less chance of being spotted. The moon on this cloudless night lit his way.

Unknown to him a farmer, old Mr. Kelly, was out to bring his dog in for the night when he spotted Timmy walking past. He thought it strange to see a young lad walking down the road at that late hour. The lad was in the shadow of the trees so he couldn't make out who it might be, but he did have a sneaking suspicion it might be Timmy

O'Neill. *'Now where could he have come from?'* he thought to himself.

When Timmy reached the village, all was quiet. The pubs were closed and there was no one in the streets. He made his way cautiously towards his Dad's house, taking care to stay in the shadows. When he got there he waited several minutes, working up the courage to knock on the door. He had rehearsed over and over again in his mind what he would say. He was nervous as hell.

After several seconds prevaricating, he banged on the door. The house was a bit apart from neighbouring houses so he hoped no one else would hear. A minute or two later he heard some shuffling and a light came on. His Dad's voice came from behind the door: "Who's that banging at this late hour? I've a good mind to call the Guards."

Timmy took a deep breath before replying: "It's Timmy, Dad. I know I have some explaining to do."

Timmy's voice was muffled through the door and Mícheál Óg wasn't at all sure it could be him. "What kind of a sick prank is this? Timmy disappeared three months ago. Only last week he was presumed dead and the Guards opened a possible murder file."

"Dad, it's really me. I can explain."

"You have exactly one minute to tell me something that only Timmy could know. Don't bother with date of birth, exam results, or anything else that is easily discovered." Although Mícheál Óg now felt it was Timmy's voice, he still couldn't be sure with the distortion. He was so afraid of being deceived, being conned, that he dared not immediately open the door.

Timmy pondered a moment, then started: "You remember how we would always watch movies together. One of us would choose from the hundreds of DVDs in the spare bedroom. And that time when I was 10 or 11 when I had to go to the dentist and I came back a bundle of nerves. You told me to cheer up, that I had had an anaesthetic, and that if I had even the slightest inkling of how bad a dentist's drill could be without an anaesthetic, I would not have carried on the way I did. That evening you selected the movie 'Marathon Man' from your collection, without any indication of what was to come. Until the scene where Dustin Hoffman was strapped into the chair, being interrogated by Laurence Olivier, with the dentist's drill as an implement of torture. You turned to me and said: *'that's real dental pain.'* I started crying and said I would never again complain about a visit to the dentist."

Now it was Micheál Óg's turn to weep. He had been hoping against hope that this moment would arrive. He opened the door, reached out, and father and son embraced. After what seemed like an age, his Dad led Timmy inside and closed the door.

Once inside, Timmy broke down and cried. He was sobbing inconsolably and could hardly talk. His Dad told him about the horror experienced by John-Joe and Fergie at his sudden disappearance, that he had literally disappeared before their eyes. And how despite the trauma, they had the courage to call immediately to Micheál Óg with the awful news. And the days and weeks combing the area, divers searching the lake, before eventually they had no option to pronounce Timmy missing, presumed dead.

Timmy, still sobbing and unable to talk about what had happened those past three months, began to talk about how he needed to get a new identity. "I can't just appear and say I have spent the last three months in Bay Lough. I'd be locked up," he sobbed. "I need to find a new identity and disappear from around here."

He remembered from another movie *'The Day of the Jackal'* how the assassin wandered around a cemetery looking for the gravestone of a boy, any boy, who died in infancy somewhere close to his own birth date. He applied for a birth cert in that name, and later applied for a passport. Micheál Óg was not so sure. He felt it would be an unwarranted and wrong intrusion into the life of a family who had tragically lost a child in infancy.

"But I must do something," said Timmy. "I don't want to end up in gaol or in the mental asylum."

Mícheál Óg could well appreciate the difficulties ahead, but more importantly he was worried about Timmy, that he wasn't talking about what had happened to him. After a few minutes he said: "Let's just take a walk to clear our heads in the night air. There will be nobody around at this hour to see us."

Off they went, walking silently, each enjoying the company of the other they had so missed. Timmy gradually seemed to be calming down, but his Dad let the silence continue, waiting until Timmy was ready to talk. Soon, without ever having decided where they were going, they found themselves on the old road which led up towards Bay Lough and almost before they knew it, they were on the shores of the lake. It was a beautiful sight on that clear moonlit night.

"Show me what happened," asked Mícheál Óg. Timmy showed him where he dived in, how he had suddenly been pulled under in the middle of the lake, and where he suspected John-Joe and Fergie were at that time. "Exactly as John-Joe and Fergie told the story," said Mícheál Óg. "They were devasted, tended to blame themselves somehow although they had no reason to feel any guilt."

Then, for the first time, Timmy started to talk. "I was pulled down by this beautiful woman who called herself Niamh. She told me I was in Tír na Óg."

Mícheál Óg thought this was fantastical: Tír na nÓg under Bay Lough? Had Timmy lost the run of himself? Had he lost his mind? Was he delusional? He was seriously concerned for his sanity.

But yet, he thought, hadn't he warned Timmy about the dangers, even citing the legend of Petticoat Loose? Was that any less unreal than Tír ne n Óg? The whole episode had been so strange, with Timmy seemingly having disappeared from the face of the earth, that maybe the only explanation was that this was the truth?

He looked at the water and a thought came to him. By returning to Tír na Óg, they could avoid any and all problems of explanations and identity. He looked at Timmy with raised eyebrows and nodded towards the lake. Timmy saw it and understood immediately what was on his mind. He screamed:

"No Dad, you can't! You can't risk being pulled under."

Mícheál Óg taken aback by the panic in Timmy's scream, replied calmly: "Why not? Surely Tír na nÓg is our best option. We could avoid the valley of squinting windows whispering about your sanity and mine for the rest of our lives."

Timmy hadn't even begun to tell his Dad about all that had happened, but before he could say another word, even though there wasn't a puff of wind, a ripple drifted across the surface of the lake. First a hand appeared, then a head of hair and then a young woman emerged. Niamh. Or Petticoat Loose in the guise of Niamh.

"**NOOO!**" screamed Timmy, with a look of horror on his face.

"Yes," she answered with a smile, stretching out both arms.

Just as Mícheál Óg was about to grasp one of her hands, Timmy grabbed a hold of him and dragged him back. "**NO DAD, DON'T!**" he cried out.

Mícheál Óg was bewildered and wondered what Timmy was on about. Surely this was the answer they were looking for? They could live together in this wonderland for as long as they wanted.

Then, before Timmy could say another word, another beautiful young girl emerged from the water. Deirdre. She spoke to Timmy: "Oh Timmy I'm so glad you came back, and with your Dad. Now you can both come down to Tír na nÓg. I was so looking forward to this moment."

Timmy looked at her in disgust. Whatever doubt he may have harboured, it was clear now that she too was part of the plot. And to think he had been falling for her.

"Go away Deirdre or whoever you are. You sicken me," he said in a resigned tone. She wasn't even worth shouting at, he thought.

Niamh wasn't giving up. She spoke directly to Mícheál Óg in her soft sweet voice: "Oh, don't take any notice of Timmy, he'll come round in a minute. He's just a bit confused having left us so recently and afraid to admit his true feelings for Deirdre. You know she asked especially to come with me tonight to see Timmy again. Take my hand and discover the delights that young Timmy has enjoyed for the last three months."

Timmy knew exactly what he was doing. "Dad, I haven't even started my story. Yes, that woman you see is the same woman who dragged me down and called herself Niamh from Tír na nÓg, but that's not who she really is. And yes that girl beside her is Deirdre who so enchanted me below. I don't know who she is or what she has to do with Niamh, but I can assure you nothing good will ever come from either of them. There's so much more to tell and it is anything but good. I really enjoyed our quiet walk together, it has given me time to calm down and be able to think clearly. But however appealing you might think it is, we're not going down there. Listen to me and you'll soon realise exactly why."

All the time, Timmy maintained an ironclad grip on Mícheál Óg to keep him well back from the water's edge. Now that there was no possible doubt that Niamh was the Petticoat Loose of legend, he knew she couldn't stray more than twenty or thirty paces from Bay Lough, where she had been banished by that Bishop some 700 years previously.

Mícheál Óg now turned his back on Petticoat Loose and said to Timmy; "I don't know what's going on here Timmy, but I trust you over those two women, however charming and inviting they may be. Let's walk back to the house and you can tell me everything. If going into the lake is the good deal I think it is, it will still be available tomorrow. If not, it is as well to pass on it."

Well, on hearing that, Niamh dispensed with her role and showed herself as Petticoat Loose. Knowing she had lost the battle she flew into a rage, and with a loud shrieking voice shouted: "Don't either of you two ever think of swimming in Bay Lough if you know what's good for you. **Ever. Ever. Ever!**"

Mícheál Óg turned around and now saw the evil and spiteful witch she really was before she and Deirdre vanished into the waters of Bay Lough and back to their underworld below.

Father and son walked back to the house in silence. Once inside, Timmy started talking.

"You remember Dad when Granny was in the nursing home? She was there for three years in a warm and comfortable place, well taken care of, good food, medical treatment when required. But there was one thing missing, as you remarked on more than one occasion. Nothing seemed to bring a smile to her face, nothing got her excited. You were so sad that this was her fate. I was quite young, but I sensed that too. She was there, just waiting to die.

"Well, my experience of that so-called Tír na nÓg reminded me of that. Not initially of course where I was charmed by what appeared to be the beautiful life there. But afterwards. I began to notice the same signs on the faces of people down there. They seemed vaguely content but they weren't truly alive.

"At first, I only knew the woman who brought me there as Niamh of Tír na nÓg, so different from the Petticoat Loose of legend.

"I thought about the possibility that we might decide to go there. However, that quickly faded when I became aware of the disinterest, the lethargy of all the other people down there. I began to see it as something like a comfort blanket, a drug if you must, that would eventually choke off any zest for life we might have. But more importantly, in time I came to realise that the whole underworld was an evil trap. Tír na nÓg it most certainly wasn't."

Timmy noticed a wall chart where his Dad had been ticking off the days since he went missing. It showed he had been missing for exactly three months. But if time had been suspended for the first three days, it should have been no more than two months and twenty-eight days! So that story of not being missed for three days was another ruse to give him comfort for those initial days. And it worked. He told his Dad about this, saying, "Everything about so-called 'Tír na nÓg' was a delusion."

He told him about all the inconsistencies that came to him while walking earlier that day, how it became clear to him that whatever doubts he might have had, he could not have been in Tír na nÓg.

"When you told me to be careful about swimming across Bay Lough, I really had no idea why, and I don't think you had either, Dad. Did you really?"

"No," his Dad replied, "not really. I suppose it's just what dad's say to their children all the time: *be careful!*"

Timmy continued. He told of how Niamh had delayed him for vital seconds so that he missed the three day deadline, and how confusing he found it that such a seemingly wondrous place would keep him captive against his will, "all for a few stupid seconds". How Deirdre had captivated him with her beauty and charm on their long days out on horseback. How at the critical time as he was going to tell Manannán he was leaving on the three month deadline, she came to him and pleaded with him to stay. However much he was tempted, he knew he must return to Clogheen. But what they had just seen up at the lake tonight marked her clearly as a stooge of Petticoat Loose.

"The people down there seemed to change all the time. Except for Deirdre, I never met the same people twice. Why? Where had they gone? All so very strange.

"There was once a fleeting moment when I saw Manannán and Niamh, not as beautiful people, but as evil old hag and son, but it was so fleeting, that I doubted what I saw.

"But as you witnessed tonight up at Bay Lough, when that woman saw I was resisting her charm, and that I was convincing you to resist her, she flew into a rage and displayed her true nature. She is indeed the wicked Petticoat Loose of the legend.

"But enough of that. I have to decide how I can get back to normality without being locked away somewhere. And I do mean to get my life back. You were right, it would be an intrusion into the privacy of some family to try and steal their child's identity. I have no option but to go with the truth, whatever the consequences. I don't want to hide away for the rest of my life."

VI

The very next day, at about half past ten in the morning, Mícheál Óg and Timmy walked down the main street of Clogheen and into the Garda Station. Heads were turned:

"Is that Timmy O'Neill? I thought he was dead. Where did he appear from?"

"Who's that with Mícheál Óg O'Neill? It couldn't be his son, could it?"

"If I'm not mistaken, that's Timmy O'Neill with Mícheál Óg. I wonder if John-Joe and Fergie know he's back?"

Old Mrs. Manahan, who had just had one of her many sleepless nights, had seen a young man walking in the shadows sometime after the pubs closed. Now, next morning she saw Mícheál Óg and Timmy walking down the town and felt sure it was Timmy she had seen. She said so to her carer, adding: *'Now where did he come from?'*

All the small town speculation and gossip you would expect.

At the Garda Station, Garda McCluskey, on desk duty that day, looked up, rubbed his eyes and looked again. "Young man, if you're who I think you are, you have some explaining to do. Name please."

"Timmy O'Neill."

"That's what I thought. Do you have any idea of what you put me and my colleagues through these past three months? Not to mention your father and those two young lads, John-Joe and Fergie. You better have a bloody good explanation, young man."

Timmy started talking and at first McCluskey started to take notes. But as the full story started to emerge, he put down his pen, folded his arms and listened in disbelief. A few moments later he interrupted: "Do you really expect me to believe that gibberish? I don't know whether to lock you up or call in a psychiatrist. Or both."

Mícheál Óg spoke. "Garda McCluskey, believe it or not, my son is telling the truth. I'll vouch for that. He's here to declare that due to circumstances beyond his control, he was absent this world for a time but is now back. He's here to declare that contrary to being dead as suspected, he's very much alive. We are quite happy to undergo a DNA test to prove this, though I find it hard to see the need for this. I understand your difficulty in coming to terms with this. Only a few short hours ago, I had the same difficulty myself. So perhaps, instead of calling a psychiatrist, you might call a doctor and get him to do what's necessary to prove he is my son.

"As regards locking him up, I don't know what crime you think he may be guilty of, because I don't see any. The manner of his disappearance is to say the least unorthodox, but to my knowledge, there is no crime in taking off somewhere for a while without alerting the Guards."

Garda McCluskey was flummoxed, he had no answer to that.

Instead he said, "Timmy O'Neill present yourself here tomorrow morning at ten to have a DNA sample taken. You too Mr. O'Neill."

As soon as the two had left the station he took up the phone to call Garda Headquarters in Dublin to tell them what had happened and to seek advice as to how to proceed.

The crowd in Dublin initially thought this was some sort of a joke, but eventually engaged. Had this young man deceived anyone? No. Had he robbed anything and absconded? No. Had he assaulted anyone? No. In fact every question asked to try and elicit whether a crime might have been committed received the same answer – "No!"

Having thus established that there was no evidence of a crime, they ventured into the question of his sanity. Was he nervous or unsettled? No more than you would expect of anyone coming into a Garda Station to report something. Was his story consistent? Yes. Did he think his father believed him? Yes. Apart from the strangeness of his story, was there any other reason or sign to suggest he might be a little bit mad? No.

Detective Feeney finished by saying: "It's certainly a strange story, the likes of which I have never come across before. But I don't see you have any reason to hold or charge him. I'd say the best you could do would be to ask the doctor to probe the young man while taking the DNA sample, to see if he detects any sign of insanity."

"OK," said Garda McCluskey. "One last thing: what about charging him with obstruction or wasting Garda time?"

"From what you told me, I can't see how he could be guilty of obstruction or wasting your time. As a sixteen year old young man, he was entitled to go wherever he wanted without saying anything to anyone. Unless you think the father was in on it and you wanted to charge him, which I doubt very much. No, the best thing you can do is leave it lie and let him deal with it with his friends and the people of Clogheen, however be sees fit."

"OK, thanks," said McCluskey, very much in a resigned tone of voice, as he put down the phone. "Now, who'll believe me when I go home this evening?" he thought to himself, shaking his head.

The doctor took the DNA samples next morning, which in time proved if proof were needed they were father and son. He asked a few probing questions of Timmy, but he seemed sane enough.

John-Joe and Fergie soon found out Timmy was back. The three lads got together, all delighted to see one another, although there was no shortage of incredulity at Timmy's story.

The pubs in Clogheen were buzzing with excitement at the news that Timmy was back – alive! The old farmer, Mr. Kelly was for once the centre of attention when he declared he was the first to spot Timmy that night as he walked down from Bay Lough. Even Mrs. Manahan convinced her carer to bring her to the pub for the first time in God knows how many years. She too wanted to tell her story.

The talk of the town took a different turn when Timmy's story to Garda McCluskey leaked out, for, in all fairness, who could expect such an amazing story to be kept confidential?

A few brash young-fellows boasted that THEY would have no problem swimming across the lake. They gathered a crowd the next day and duly did just that. There was no stopping them, afterwards declaring: *'We dared Petticoat Loose and she was afraid to take us on!'* They even went so far as to have T-shirts printed with:

COME OUT NOW PETTICOAT LOOSE!
SHOW YOURSELF!

But of course she didn't.

Next Sunday the Church was fuller than usual for Mass. The

Parish priest made sure in his sermon to warn about the evils of witches and devils. He announced that he would lead a procession to Bay Lough that evening to bless the lake and banish Petticoat Loose forever. Over 100 parishioners followed him.

However, word spread like wildfire that an exorcism of the lake would be performed that evening and there must have been at least another 5,000 people from near and far turned up to see what it was all about. There was much shouting and cameras were flashing as people crowded towards the front. Fr. Byrne decided he would not repeat that procession.

Then there was the doomsday crowd. Well, hardly a crowd, it consisted of just one: Jerry North and his placard parading around the town, hoping to gather some supporters. Alas, there were none.

The conversation in the pubs changed from the safe return of Timmy to the relentless pursuit of theories to explain away the appearance of Petticoat Loose, or whoever or whatever it was that had detained Timmy for three months.

In time the pubs returned to their long established role as that great social institution where everyone is an expert on sport, politics and the problems of the world. Life was back to normal in Clogheen.

VII

For Mícheál Óg and Timmy, getting back to normal was not so easy. While they continued to go quietly about their day to day lives, vivid and troubling memories remained.

Timmy would sometimes wake up in the middle of the night in a sweat after a recurring nightmare where he saw himself as one of those aimless and listless people trapped forever in Petticoat Loose's twilight zone. In time the frequency and intensity of his trauma did ease, but never fully left him.

Micheál Óg for his part was forever haunted by how close he had come to grasping Niamh's, or should I say Petticoat Loose's hand, that fateful night beside the lake.

Occasionally Timmy and his Dad stroll up to Bay Lough, taking care to stand well back as they ponder those events that could so easily have ended in disaster.

*   *   *

Whether Fr. Byrne's blessing of the lake actually resulted in the banishment of Petticoat Loose remains a moot point. All we can say is that there hasn't been another case since. At least that we know of.

But as for tomorrow or some other day off into the future, who knows what might happen? Only time will tell.

Butter

I

Butter, that quintessential dairy product so prized in Ireland and in all corners of the globe for cooking and baking, and worthy of its rightful place on the table at meal-time. It even makes its way into literature and I have in mind that great Joycean work, so impenetrable to many, *Finnegan's Wake*.

My trip to the charming town of Silkeborg in Denmark sometime back in the 1990s was to visit the dairy equipment company *Pasilac*. As a visiting Irishman, my host drew my attention to a plaque in the foyer which featured a quotation from *Finnegan's Wake*:

> *Now, while I am not out now to be taken up as*
> *unintentionally recommending the **Silkebjorg***
> *tyrondynamon machine for the more economical helixtrolysis*
> *of these amboadipates until I can find space to look into it*
> *myself a little more closely...*

In the early 20th century the company had been called *Silkeborg Maskinfabrik* and was famous for its butter making machines, of which there were many in Ireland. That James Joyce saw fit to mention their company in his book was a matter of great pride.

We take the ready availability of butter for granted. In times of scarcity, however, satisfying our desire for that quintessential product may require a degree of ingenuity. As we shall see...

II

L iz lived in London. By September 1940 Londoners were subjected to systematic bombing by the Luftwaffe. On top of that, due to the scarcity of many food items, they had to live with rationing.

Liz's friend May lived in Clonmel in Ireland. They wrote regularly to one another.

Knightsbridge, London
24ᵗʰ October 1940

My dear May,

Life here continues to be so frightening with all the bombs the Germans have been dropping on us for over a month now. Every time we hear the air raid sirens, we rush to the nearest underground station which is used as a bomb shelter. It's so crushed and crowded down there, but it does provide a safe place for us. After the 'all clear' we go back up above ground. Only then can we see the trail of destruction left behind.

But the resilience of the people here is amazing. If Herr Hitler expects to destroy the dogged grit of the English and beat them into submission, he is so mistaken. People here are more and more determined that they will not be vanquished.

How I long for the peace that must reign in Clonmel. In comparison with the awful nightly threats of bombs, some of my own little problems are truly insignificant. But most of all, I miss being able to bake a cake, or smother the potatoes in butter. With butter rationed to 2 oz. a week and the appalling quality of flour in the shops, there's little chance of that.

But enough of me. You must tell me all about how life continues under your 'emergency' back in Clonmel.

Yours affectionately,

Liz

May replied in due course:

Clonmel,

3rd November 1940

My dear Liz,

I was so delighted to receive your letter and to know that you are safe. We do know that the Germans are bombing London, but get few enough details. The censors are very diligent, though I can't for the life of me understand why it matters one iota whether or what we know about the bombings.

I don't know if I told you, but in July the Local Security Force got word that the Germans were about to land at Dungarvan, and on the fair day here too. They had to cancel the fair day and no one was happy about that. Thank God there was no invasion.

Then at the end of August a German warplane dropped some bombs on Campile in County Wexford, killing three women working in the local co-op. An accident they said, but tragic and all too real. Rather too close for comfort, less than 100 miles from Clonmel. Please God there will be no more of those 'accidents'.

Mr. DeValera is recruiting an awful lot of men into the army to be able to withstand an invasion. It would seem that Mr. Churchill would like to take back the ports of Cobh, Berehaven and Swilly, so recently restored to us. The word is that he will agree to unite the country if we back England and allow access to the ports. No one here believes that. There would be uproar if we backed England's war, so I don't think that will happen. The talk now is that Churchill might invade and take the ports by force if we don't comply.

Worrying times! But I just may be able to help out with butter. Leave it with me and I'll see what I can do.

Your dear friend,
May

There was butter rationing in Ireland too, but May found a way around that. A month later, Liz received a parcel. Inside was a sponge cake, and concealed within was a pound of butter flattened out between two sheets of grease-proof paper. She couldn't believe her luck. She immediately put pen to paper.

Knightsbridge, London,
7th November 1940

My Dear May,

What a lovely surprise I got when I opened your parcel this morning. Tell me how did you do it? You can't believe what a thrill it was to receive the butter. And the cake, how did you manage to bake it? The flour here is so coarse that baking cakes is out of the question. Is it easy to get nice flour in Ireland? You must tell me everything.

Yours affectionately,
Liz

May replied:

Conmel,
12th November 1940

My dear Liz,

I'm so glad the cake arrived. I was afraid the customs people would discover the butter and confiscate the lot. We have butter rationing here too, but with the butcher's shop I have lots of contact with farmers, many of whom churn their own butter. Since they have no need of coupons, I managed to prevail on a few of them to give me some of theirs.

As regards the flour, the truth is that the flour here is very coarse, no better than yours in England, I'm sure. My secret ingredient is a miller's silk sieve which I managed to acquire. Sieve the flour with this and what passes through is quite good enough.

Here talk of English and German invasions seems to have faded. I don't know if that's because the risks have gone away or because the censors are being more diligent in denying us news.

Lots of our young men are heading to England to enlist in the British army. I think it's as much to earn money as to support England's war effort. I often wonder how many will make it back.

Your dear friend,
May

III

For the duration of the war and afterwards until rationing finally ended in 1954, May would regularly send a cake and a pound of butter to Liz, adding a bit of sparkle to her life. For all their vigilance the customs officials never found the contraband.

In the summer of 1955 May finally got to travel to London again. The two friends had a warm-hearted reunion, everything you would expect following their separation during those difficult years. Greetings over, they sat down to afternoon tea. A sponge cake, freshly baked with butter, filled and topped with whipped cream and fresh strawberries.

"It was the least I could do to say thank you for all those cakes and pounds of butter," Liz said as she cut a slice for May and poured the tea.

Mikey

I

A ge takes its toll. It creeps up on you without your noticing. Little things: you find you're a bit stiffer in the joints, a bit slower in some things, but you brush it off. You're fine really. You decide to exercise a bit more. Maybe go to the gym or take up Yoga or Pilates. They help you out. You're really OK.

But as you move from your fifties to your sixties, then your seventies and on to your eighties, inexorably but surely you come to realise your time on this earth is finite. And you find yourself going to more funerals as your friends and acquaintances are being picked off one by one by the grim reaper.

So it was that in my 85th year, now living alone, my doctor said I really did need to consider some form of assisted living.

"You mean a nursing home, I suppose," I replied with more than a hint of displeasure.

"Yes, that's exactly what I mean, Frank," he replied. "Take a look at yourself: you're not eating properly or taking care of yourself. Why don't I get a community nurse to call to you? She'll be better able to explain everything to you. No obligation. Whatever you do will be your decision."

He spoke some truth, but I didn't want to acknowledge it. However, I relented: "OK, get this young do-gooder to call to me. I promise to be civil, but no more than that."

The end result was that some three months later I found myself heading for the "Smiling Eyes Care Home". I don't know why they bother with those catchy names – everybody knows it makes no difference to what goes on inside. But I had chosen it for its location – not so far from the home town of my youth and in view of Slievenamon. For my final days, however long that might be, I wanted to return to that familiar place. A nostalgia trip for sure.

I was brought to my room – basic enough: bed, chair, small *en-suite* bathroom, a desk, a TV and an extra chair for a visitor. I was glad to see they had managed to grant my request for a room with a view of Slievenamon.

I was shown to the day room to meet some of the other residents. I knew what to expect: people sitting down, television in the corner - some talking, reading or knitting; others no longer having the interest or energy.

I looked around, wondering if I might recognise anyone from the long gone days of my youth. For a while it seemed not, but I was stopped in my tracks when I saw Mikey O'Connor sitting down, engrossed in a book. I had to look twice to make sure it was him, after all it had been nearly seventy years since I had last set eyes on him.

II

Before I go any further, I should tell you a bit about Mikey. He was around the same age as myself. We sat side by side in the Convent school when we were four years old and for a few years more as we went up through the classes. But Mikey, God help us, was not the full shilling – a term we used back then but no longer appropriate. Still, I tell it as it was.

Over the years he kept being held back a class until eventually he left school altogether at age about twelve, as far as I remember, and still only in 3rd Class. By that stage the rest of us were in 6th Class and looking towards secondary school.

His speech was very difficult to understand, and when you did manage to make out what he was saying, it never seemed to amount to much. I didn't think he had ever learned to read or write, hence my surprise at seeing him engrossed in a book.

After he left school, he ended up as a messenger boy with a local butcher. Those who were well got – and back then having a phone in the house was part of that – would phone the butcher in the morning, give their order, and await delivery by Mikey on his messenger boy's bicycle.

He did well in that job, surprisingly enough myself and a few others thought. I mean, how could he read the address for delivery? Or know where to go? No doubt, in time there were the repeat deliveries to the same customers. But how did he get to know who everyone was? No matter, rightly or wrongly that was how we young-fellows thought.

The messenger boy era came to an end and Mikey was just one of those characters about town, unemployed and unemployable. Some years later, around the time I headed off looking for greener pastures, he seemed to disappear. Where to, we had no idea.

III

I went over to him. Before saying a word I looked at the book and noted that it was the right way up, a fifty-fifty chance I supposed. "Hello. Mikey O'Connor, if I'm not mistaken?" He looked up, mumbled some sort of reply, and returned to his book.

Clearly he had no interest in talking to me, that is even if he had recognised me, so I found a seat elsewhere. Afterwards I occasionally saluted him in passing, but he just mumbled something before continuing. I had little expectation of further engagement.

But one day out of the blue that all changed. It was after breakfast and I was heading to one of the sitting rooms when Mikey came up to me. Boy, was I in for a big surprise.

He gripped my arm in the way that only older people do, before saying: "Frank Meagher, let's sit down a while," as he guided me to a chair and signalled for me to sit beside him.

We sat down. I was speechless. Was this really the Mikey I remembered? The look on my face, no doubt, said it all.

"Frank," he continued, "That first day you came up to me, you were wondering about the fact that I was sitting down reading a book, perhaps even considering whether it was just some sort of prop. It's OK, I understand why. I was taken aback somewhat when you recognised me after more than sixty years. It has taken me a little time to come around to the possibility of having this conversation, which would have been impossible those long years ago when we first knew one another."

I took my time before replying: "Mikey, you're right, that's exactly what was going through my mind when I first saw you here. All I can say is that it is both a surprise to know that you have somehow over the years gotten control over your speech and your learning, as well as a delight to see this has happened. Please forgive my disbelief. I really am happy for you. If I'm not being too intrusive, I would be honoured if you would tell me how it all came about."

"It's a long story, Frank, and to be truthful few enough people know it. I suppose at this late stage in life, I should tell it. In any case, it will help break the monotony of this place. With neither of us likely to be going anywhere, there'll be time enough. I hope I won't bore you."

It was indeed quite a story which stretched credulity to breaking point many a time. He started by saying I was the first person to recognise him since his arrival. He had lived most of his life away from here and only returned when the Nursing Home beckoned because, just like myself, he wanted to end his days where he could see Slievenamon.

What follows is Mikey's story as it emerged slowly over many days, interrupted by cups of tea, afternoon naps, nursing home programme etc. As much as possible, I will try to use his own words.

IV

Mikey's parents were of course delighted with their new born son. In the early years everything seemed to be going well. But then they began to notice that his first baby-talk words were not developing into the speech of an older child. Physically, he seemed to be OK, but not hugely agile as he progressed from taking baby steps. This physical development they put down to the simple fact that some children are more agile and athletic than others, and that he was unlikely to develop into a sports star. That didn't unduly worry them. But the speech did.

"They discussed my development with the local GP. He saw me a few times and concluded that I was somewhat retarded. Remember this was back in the 1950s and specialists were out of range for people with a poor or humble background.

"In any case, my parents accepted what the doctor told them and hoped that over time there would be some improvement. Just before my fifth birthday, I started school – that's when we got to know one another, Frank, when we were put sitting side by side.

"I remember Sister Assumpta was teaching us through low and high infants. She was kindly enough and in truth as I recollect, she spent a disproportionate amount of time with me, but in time realised – or at least thought – not much was getting through to me.

"Let me tell you now, believe it or not, I was a sponge for all the learning and knowledge coming to me, but it was a one way process. I could understand everything, even better than others, I think. But I had no way of getting it back out again. Try as I might, my speech impediment got in the way and I was unable to signal my understanding. My handwriting was at best a scrawl and the subject of much derision by others in the class, you included I suppose."

At this I interjected: "Yes, Mikey, I must admit I was one of those. I hope at this late stage you can accept my apology."

"Apology accepted," Mikey continued. "I can understand the circumstances and I hold no grudge. Later, as you know, I was kept back a class on a few occasions, not that it made one iota of difference. If truth be known, the only reason I was kept in school at all was due to the persistence of my parents. The school relented time and again.

"The constant taunting by other boys and girls made me turn in on myself. The one thing I clung to was that despite that everyone else thought I was a bit of an imbecile, I knew and understood the world as well or better than any of you. I soaked up everything and kept hoping that some day it would all change.

"But it didn't. Everything remained a one-way flow. I received all the knowledge and understanding but could not communicate that to anyone. At 12 years of age and still only in third class, I left school. I managed to get my parents to understand that I wouldn't go back, and God knows, they had lost all hope of a change in me by this time. They had little enough money themselves, so they looked around for some sort of a job that would keep me occupied and bring in a few shillings to the family.

"In time they managed to convince the butcher, Mr. McCarthy, to take me on as a messenger boy. Inside my head, in that part of me unable to express myself, I was determined to make this work. And I think Mr. McCarthy was surprised and pleased to discover I was reliable and quick in delivering meat parcels to customers. And I also think that the customers, initially somewhat surprised that their orders always got to them in time, grew to trust me. At Christmas I would often get a small present. A few discovered when my birthday fell and would slip me a few bob.

"Most of all, my parents were delighted that this was going well, and that I was bringing some badly needed money into the house.

"Sometime towards the end of the 60s, as you will recall Frank, work for messenger boys dried up. More and more people had cars and did their own shopping. Mr. McCarthy had no option but to let me go.

"At this point, I was unemployed and unemployable, dependent on the dole. The dole office called me in from time to time to see about getting me a job, however their heart wasn't in it. They were just going through the motions. They had no faith in my employability, and I suppose they could hardly be blamed."

Often enough Mikey would turn to me: "Frank, I hope I'm not boring you with this stuff, most of which you no doubt remember from our youth" I came to realise that he was signalling he was tired and we would take a break for a nap, to watch TV, or turn in for the night. Occasionally it might be a day or two before our conversation resumed. Neither of us was exactly full of energy and these conversations – they were really more like monologues – must have been draining for Mikey. I got to understand that telling it was important for him, that he was in some way unburdening himself, that it was a form of catharsis to have it all out in the open. I never once had to prompt him to continue.

"Where did we leave off yesterday?" he would often ask me, before recalling himself exactly where he had finished. In time, the full story was revealed.

He survived on the dole, living at home, nothing to do all day except wander around. A few of those to whom he had delivered meat were aware of his situation and would sometimes slip him a few shillings, or even occasionally a ten shilling or pound note.

He started hanging around the bookies office, but they all knew him and wouldn't take a bet, probably not least, he said, because they had no way of being sure what horse he was trying to bet on.

"You'll remember this, Frank. I took a notion that I would like to swim in the river. Yourself and a few of your friends used to swim a few times a week and one day I saw you all there. I managed to explain by gestures that I wanted to swim too but had no swimming togs. You all started talking among yourselves, mostly worrying that I might drown, and then what would you do? Eventually you relented and I jumped in. You must admit Frank, I was a natural."

"You were, Mikey," I replied. "Completely unexpected but you were as good as any of us. Better even, because later, when we got the courage to jump in from the Convent bridge – it must be 20 or 25 feet over the water – you were the only one to dive in head first. The rest of us just jumped in feet first. You became a bit of a legend."

"I did, didn't I?" he continued with a smile.

"It wasn't long after that when a decisive event happened which was to change my life. If I remember correctly, it was around the time you went off somewhere to study or find a career for yourself."

At this point I interrupted. "That must have been when I took the £10 assisted passage to Australia. There wasn't much by way of jobs or careers available in Ireland back then. I spent over 35 years out there."

"You must tell me about that sometime," Mikey continued before getting back to his own story. "I'm sure you've come across colourfully dressed South Americans playing the pan pipes. Well there was a group of them playing on the street one day just there near the Main Guard. As I walked past I started to dance something like a jig, I'm sure not in any way appropriate for that music, or possibly any music! But it caught the attention of one of them, who came over and spoke to me, his English was reasonably good.

"'Tell me about your dance,' he said. 'Is this some sort of traditional Irish dance?'

"I responded with some sort of guttural tone and gestured, pointing to my mouth and ears, indicating I couldn't answer him. I thought that would be the end of that, but after reflecting for a moment or two, he continued.

"'Is this some problem from when you were born? Or from an accident?'

"Surprised at his engagement, I put my hand out and gradually lowered it to the ground, indicating, I hoped, that I was like this since birth. He was quiet for a few moments, he seemed deep in thought. His friends stopped playing the pan pipes and were now paying attention to his engagement with me. Then he spoke again.

"'Severe communication disorder," he said. *'A good brain but unable to find a way of expressing what you want to say. Your thoughts, your feelings, are trapped inside for lack of communication ability.'*

This was a mind-blowing experience for Mikey. For the first time in his life, a total stranger had seen immediately where the problem was, that he wasn't retarded or stupid, just that his body didn't work properly, he couldn't communicate. He was able to walk and cycle and swim and carry out ordinary physical acts. But he just couldn't engage with others. Something was missing.

"The pan pipes player saw the smile on my face and he smiled back. My first ever communication with a foreigner. But more was to come from this stranger.

"'You must come with me to the Altiplano, the land of my ancestors. We know how to cure this,' he said.

"I didn't know what to think. Who was this man? Could I trust him? Of course I was living with my parents. What would they think of this stranger? I had no idea where this Altiplano, or the land of his ancestors was, much less who those ancestors might be. How would I get there? Who would pay? And if I did go there, what would they do to me? More likely Dadda would call the Guards rather than let that man take me away.

"But, as you might imagine, I was intrigued with the possibility that this man might hold the key to my life, my future. I managed to gesture that he should accompany me home. There were four of them in the pan-pipes band, but only the man who had spoken came with me. When Mamma saw him, being the welcoming woman she was, she invited him in and offered him a cup of tea, while at the same time Dadda looked at me with raised eyebrows. Who was this stranger, an obvious foreigner, that I had brought to the house?

"Tea was served and the interrogation began. The easy part was the exchange of names. Then the question of where he was from. *'I am a descendent of an ancient race, from before the time of the Inca, from the Altiplano in the Andes.'*

"'*I've heard of the Andes,'* Dadda said. *'They're somewhere in South America. But I never heard of a country called Altiplano. Where exactly is it?'*

"My friend responded: *'Altiplano isn't the name of a country, rather it is a vast plane high up in the Andes, which spans a number of modern day countries. However, we don't recognise the artificial boundaries created by these countries, which are no more than the result of fighting and squabbling among the Conquistadores in their wars to secure independence from Spain.'*

"As you might imagine, this did not satisfy Dadda at all. Whatever about the past and the Conquistadores, there were countries there now and he had to be from one of them. But try as he might, my friend refused to bow and that impasse remained unresolved.

"Next of course was the question of why he came home with me. *'Your boy stopped to listen to our music in the street and started to dance. He had a smile on his face and clearly enjoyed himself. We stopped playing and I started to talk to him and soon realised that he could not communicate. He didn't seem to be stupid or insane and it quickly became apparent to me that his brain was locked inside and that the normal functions of the body which allow the person to express themselves and communicate with others, were not working. His brain is unable to engage with the outside world. My ancestors discovered how to deal with this more than a thousand years ago, and I would like to offer your boy this treatment.'*

"This certainly did not go down well. *'Are you a qualified doctor? Where did you study medicine? In some place that isn't even a country? And you want to offer some quack treatment to my one and only son, Mikey? I don't know whether to throw you out or call the Guards. Please explain why I should pay you a blind bit of notice!'*

"Dadda had worked himself into a state. Mamma could only look on, afraid to say anything in case she made matters worse. But the mystery was how we ever got to the point where my friend had a chance to salvage the situation. I can only suggest that Dadda secretly hoped that this man might just be able to help me. Up to that moment, no one had ever even vaguely suggested my situation was capable of treatment.

"My friend took a deep breath before continuing. *'My name, Acahuana, is a royal name, for I am descended from royalty who were overthrown, dispossessed and displaced by the Spanish.*

"Dadda being a keen reader of Irish history could relate to being *'dispossessed and displaced'* in the context of the history of plantations in Ireland, and his face brightened a little. Acahuana continued:

"*'I was born in a place high in the Andes, on an island on Lake Titicaca which straddles the border between Peru and Bolivia, although we do not recognise these modern countries or borders. My family has lived in this remote place for more than a thousand years. We hold on to the ancient traditions, study them, and live by them.*

"*'You ask if I studied medicine, if I am a doctor. While it is tempting to simply say yes, this would not be of any assistance to you. Let me start by saying that my ancestors developed neurosurgery long before you here in Europe knew anything about it. Perhaps you have heard about the practice of trepanation, where a hole is cut in the skull to relieve pressure in the brain. But you might not know that by the time the Conquistadores arrived, it is accepted that trepanation performed by my ancestors had a 75% success rate, while 300 years later, during the American Civil War, the survival rate was below 50%. Now our methods have almost 100% success.*

"' What I want to offer to your son is even more advanced, was developed before the Inca conquered the Altiplano kingdom of my ancestors, and has been for centuries known only to descendants of those ancestors. The knowledge of this secret procedure is preserved within our small community who live on that remote island on Lake Titicaca.'

This, Mikey said, seemed to be an educated man speaking. However his father was surely conflicted between wanting this man to be able to do something very positive for Mikey, and the fear of allowing it to happen in case anything went wrong.

What if, instead of being the educated man he seemed to be, he were really some sort of charlatan? His father would feel personally responsible if he allowed him to perform this *'secret procedure'* and it all went wrong. Should he believe this man? Should he trust him? How much might all this cost?

"But in reality," Mikey continued, "I had no idea what he was thinking. Neither, I suspect, had Mamma. No one went to South America back then. Well, almost no one.

"Dadda left the room and went out the front door. Several minutes later he returned. I guessed he had gone to Mrs. Dillon a few doors down. She was the only one on our street with a phone back then. I presumed he went out to phone someone. But who? The Guards? Or the Parish Priest?

"Fifteen minutes later there was a knock on the door and Father O'Donnell walked in. Dadda briefly introduced him to Acahuana and gave a summary of the conversation that had transpired, before continuing: *'Father O'Donnell, you were on the missions in Peru for a few years. Did you ever come across these ancient people from the Altiplano? Did you ever hear about them performing some sort of neurosurgery with success? Should I have any faith in what this man is telling me?'*

"Father O'Donnell, ever a cautious and deliberate man, took his time before answering: *'Well, Bernard, firstly let me say that Peru is a very large and diverse country spanning a huge area from the Pacific, through the narrow coastal desert strip, to the highlands of the Altiplano and down the other side of the Andes to the Amazon basin. Our mission was on the coast centred in a city called Trujillo, hundreds of miles from the Altiplano and from the descendants of the Inca and other pre-Colombian civilisations. I did travel to the Andean highlands, the Altiplano, and visited some of the old Inca sites. They were truly an advanced society when the Spanish arrived. The Spanish conquest was more due to the diseases they brought with them, against which the local population had no natural resistance, than any military superiority. But that's all history.*

"'You ask about neurosurgery. Yes I did hear that the Inca were skilled in trepanation long before any western societies mastered the technique. It seems they drill a hole in the skull which can relieve some pressure build-up in the brain, but in truth I really know nothing about it. As to whether they were skilled in any other form of neurosurgery, I cannot say. As regards language, this man's first language is probably Quechua, not Spanish, but it seems from your description of what he was saying, that he speaks good English. No doubt you probably think that I speak fluent Spanish after my time there, but alas, I am no more than barely competent in that language.'

"'But perhaps I could have a private word with this young man, if you would permit us to go to the sitting room alone?'

"Dadda agreed and the two went off for their private conversation. There was no account of what had transpired or been discussed. But whatever the trend of their conversation, it was clear that Acahuana had convinced him of his *bona fides*.

"After this, Fr. O'Donnell said he would like to speak with a fellow priest, Fr. Bergin, who had also been in Peru, and who he felt would be rather more knowledgeable than he about the Inca and other peoples, as well as about trepanation and neurosurgery. He would come back after lunch the following day. In his conversation with Acahuana they had agreed that he would remain in town and return the next evening after tea, at around seven o'clock."

A few days later, our conversation continued.

"Where was I? Oh yes, there was this meeting about me and Acahuana. The following afternoon Fr. O'Donnell returned having spoken with Fr. Bergin. It seemed he had received some positive feedback to an extent that Dadda seemed rather upbeat about meeting Acahuana again."

The meeting happened later that evening. Mikey's father it seemed had no belief that there was any point in Mikey being there. They must have been talking for something like an hour and a half. Every now and then there were raised voices, however it did not seem that the conversation was in any way acrimonious.

Mikey continued: "When eventually the door of the sitting room opened, I was invited in. Dadda spoke to me in a slow and deliberate voice: *'Mikey, Acahuana believes he can perform an operation which will help you. I asked Fr. O'Donnell here because he has been in the country where Acahuana lives and I wanted to see whether I should trust him. Fr. O'Donnell thought a friend of his, Fr. Bergin, would be better able to judge and earlier today he spoke with him. Fr. Bergin was aware of what Acahuana proposed to do although he had no detailed knowledge of it nor had he known anyone who had undergone the procedure. Still, he was sure these people were highly honourable and felt that we could have confidence in what this man was proposing, that you would be able to communicate properly with others afterwards. Your mother and I are very nervous, but we trust Fr. O'Donnell's judgement. If you understand what I am saying, please nod your head.'*

"I was amazed. I would have tried anything. I nodded my head and made some sort of guttural sound. This Dadda took as my agreement, even though he really had little understanding of what was being proposed, much less whether I understood anything at all about it.

"But for me it was a moment of great hope: that I might at last be able to communicate with the world; that others would see me as a real person, with real thoughts and ideas; that I might have an independent life ahead of me, a career, a livelihood. I wasn't at all sure how all this might turn out, but I was excited. And I trusted blindly in Acahuana because he expressed belief in me, something I had never before experienced.

"The outcome was that I would travel with Acahuana to Lake Titicaca high up in the Andes where the operation would be performed. He would pay all my costs, but alas he could not pay for either of my parents to go with me, and they certainly did not have the wherewithal to pay for it themselves.

"I went and hugged my parents, Acahuana, and Fr. O'Donnell who seemed somewhat embarrassed with such an act of affection."

There were things to do, not least of which was to get a passport for Mikey. Fr. O'Donnell knew someone in the Department of External Affairs (this was in the years before someone in Government decided we should name change to Foreign Affairs) and said he should be able to arrange it in a week or so. Two weeks later he was ready to travel with his new passport and a ticket to Iquitos in Peru from Acahuana.

"My parents, as they saw me off, were torn between the hope that this would be a life saver for me and the fear that something awful might happen and that they might never see me again. It was a major leap in the dark for them, not knowing whether I had any idea what was in store. It was a long and very emotional goodbye."

As you, the reader, might well imagine, I was flabbergasted with the story, with the audacity of what was proposed, and the fact that a humble family man, two priests and a foreigner whom none of them knew, could end up agreeing to this wild plan. And wild it must have seemed to everyone except Acahuana. I said this to Mikey, and he agreed it was a hard story to fathom, but nonetheless it was true, he assured me. I wondered would I have had the courage to go through with such a plan if it had been my family.

V

Mikey's parents - who had never been in an airport before, much less in an aeroplane - and Fr. O'Donnell all went to Shannon Airport to see Mikey off. Many tears were shed, but eventually the flight was called, Mikey and Acahuana boarded the plane, and a short time later they took off.

The flight was to Iquitos in the Peruvian Amazon basin with an overnight stay in Miami *en route*, itself a jaw dropping experience for Mikey. Miami was hot, but in Iquitos he was exposed to the tropical heat and humidity of the Amazon, so different from anything he had ever experienced before.

They were met by a friend of Acahuana who had a small private plane. After a few stops along the way in remote places, they landed on an island on Lake Titicaca high up in the Andes, straddling the border between Peru and Bolivia.

Gone were the heat and humidity of Iquitos, and instead Mikey found himself shivering from the cold, short of breath and suffering headaches due to the thin air at that altitude. He spent much of the first few days indoors. Acahuana gave him some coca leaves to chew and told him to rest and drink plenty of water. They helped, and a few days later he was much better.

He took in his surroundings. The Island was not large and he could see water everywhere. The house was of simple, modern construction, comfortable but not grand or ostentatious. Nearby was an ancient stone building. This, Acahuana told him, was where his father lived, and his ancestors before that for generations, from long before the Spanish arrived. This was also where they would perform the neurosurgery on Mikey, but not before they were satisfied he was fully acclimatised to the altitude.

He found it all very strange. He was intrigued by the place, but also very nervous about what might come, and so lonely for home, for his parents.

Some two weeks after he arrived, he was brought to the stone building where he was introduced to Chasca (a Quechua name, after the Goddess of Dawn) who would perform the operation. Acahuana explained in great detail what was proposed, occasionally referring back to Chasca in Quechua, presumably to confirm with her that he was correct in what he said.

"The explanations were very clear and I understood well what Acahuana was saying. I nodded my understanding from time to time. But my nerves were on edge. I so much wanted this to work, and I believed that these people knew what they were doing. But what if I was wrong? What if I went through all this and ended up exactly where I had been? Or perhaps, even worse? What if I died during the procedure? Would they tell my parents? Or would they silently dispose of my body, leaving behind a mystery as to what had happened? My parents had no idea where I was, beyond being somewhere on Lake Titicaca on the vast Altiplano in the Andes

"This revolved through my mind over and over again. Mamma and Dadda really had no way of finding out what had happened if they never heard from or about me again. Except, maybe, via Fr. O'Donnell and Fr. Bergin. A scary time, but I tried not to show it.

"In any case two days after this consultation, I was brought to Chasca again. She said the time had come, if I would acknowledge that she could go ahead. Having come this far, what could I do only signal my agreement?

"Chasca gave me a potion to drink, saying that I would feel nothing during the operation. Afterwards I might feel some slight pain or discomfort, but that should fade within a week.

"I took the potion and drank it. After a few moments I started to feel all woozy, like I was floating in some ethereal space, detached from reality. I was never fully unconscious. All through the operation I had this vague perception as to what was happening. At least I think I had, but really I can't be sure what I remember and what my mind invented based on what I was told had happened.

"Sometime after the operation seemed to me to be finished, I fell into a deep, deep sleep. It must have been for the most of 24 hours, because when I came to it was early morning. I opened my eyes and looked around. I was no longer in the stone building, I was back in the room where I had been staying. I didn't sense any pain. There was a young girl in the room, and as soon as she saw me come to, she went out. A few moments later Acahuana and Chasca came in.

"*'How are you feeling now?'* asked Acahuana.

"I was afraid to open my mouth, not knowing what would emerge. Maybe my usual guttural noise. And then what? But eventually I plucked up the courage. *'I ..... feel ..... good,'* I answered, amazed I was able to speak those words. Then I continued, slowly and with great deliberation: *'I can't believe I said that. Has the operation really worked? Will I now be able to talk to people? Will they no longer think I'm just a bit stupid?'* There were smiles all round. Acahuana said the obvious: *'What you just said proves you can now talk to anyone.'*

"*'The operation was successful,'* Chasca said. *'We're really pleased it went so well.'*

"I stood up and danced a jig. Acahuana burst out laughing, turned to Chasca and said *'That's the little dance I told you about, the one that started everything.'*

"*'I can see how that captivated you,'* she replied with a smile.

At this point I interrupted Mikey and asked how he had got the news to his parents and how they responded.

"Well that wasn't so easy," he said. "You know how it was with phones back then and we certainly didn't have one. There was a microwave phone on the Island linked to a town on the shores of

Lake Titicaca. They were able to use this link to send a telegram to Dadda. Phones were few and far between, but of course Mrs. Dillon two doors down had one.

'All well. Be at Mrs. Dillon's tomorrow
2pm for a call. Mikey.'

"And that's what happened. They couldn't believe it was me. They didn't know what to say, but I could sense the delight in their voice and for me it was unreal that I was talking to them, clearly and distinctly, in my own voice."

For me too it was emotional to hear this. I asked Mikey how long he stayed there. Acahuana and Chasca had suggested he should stay a month to recover fully. He would feel a little weak after the operation, but he would gradually rebuild his strength.

"They pointed to a snow-capped mountain in the distance. *'That's Janq'u Uma[1]. If you are willing, we'll take you there in four weeks. It's not the easiest of climbs, but you are a young and fit man and you will be with experienced climbers. On a clear day, the views over Titicaca and across the Altiplano will be breath-taking. After that, you'll be ready to go home. What do you think?'*

"Of course I agreed. The mountain is about 6,500 m high. From Titicaca, where we were starting at 3,800 m, it is still quite a climb, some 2,700 m. Nearly three times the height of Carrauntoohil. There were four of us: Acahuana, myself and two experienced climbers to guide us. I had never in my life climbed a hill, much less one of the highest peaks in the Andes. They prepared me in advance by taking me on some easy local climbs. Even though by now I had become accustomed to the thin air on Lake Titicaca, these relatively easy climbs were challenging enough at first. But it really was fabulous for a small town boy in Ireland to be up there in that magnificent place. When the time came for the big climb, I was ready for it. Still,

---

[1] Ancohuma in Spanish and English

the higher we climbed the colder it got, the more difficult it became and the slower we went. But the exhilaration on reaching the top, the breath-taking views made it all worthwhile. It took us five days altogether up and down. An unbelievable experience."

Mikey fell silent for a while before continuing: "But I never did see my parents again. When we returned to the island, there was a telegram from Fr. O'Donnell waiting for me. Mamma and Dadda had been killed in a terrible accident." He fell silent again. "Everything about how my parents felt, all their hopes and expectations, their fears and anguish, I learned later from Fr. O'Donnell. He had called to them every evening after I had left."

He paused for a moment looking very tired, clearly still very upset at the memory of his parents' death. I expressed my sympathy on the loss of his parents so tragically. I told him I had heard about his parents death in a letter from my mother, but that she hadn't given any details. She wasn't much for writing long newsy letters. And I'm sure my father never wrote a letter in his life.

VI

The following day, Mikey talked about flying back to Shannon Airport. Instead of the euphoria of being back in Ireland he felt only the emptiness at the loss of his parents, that they would never share his joy, that he could never tell them how much it meant to him that they had placed their trust in Acahuana.

Fr. O'Donnell met him at Shannon Airport. The funeral had been delayed pending his return. The removal would be the next evening with the funeral mass and burial the following day. They stayed a night in a hotel near the airport, to give Mikey a chance to get over the jet-lag and to gather his thoughts before going home. Fr. Bergin was on his way to Shannon, he too very much wanted to meet Mikey.

Over dinner they had a long conversation. Mikey owed these two men so much. Without their word, his parents would never have let him go away. He heard about all the fears, hopes, and anxieties his parents had experienced. They were always on edge, hoping everything would work out but at the same time so afraid it might all go very wrong. Fr. O'Donnell must have been a great source of comfort to them, visiting every evening without fail.

Fr. Bergin asked him endless questions. He had visited several communities on the Altiplano, but had never heard of Acahuana's. He wanted to know everything about the operation, about the community on that remote island. He had been glad but also very much relieved when he heard it had all gone so well. He admitted that despite expressing confidence in Acahuana, he lived in dread of the possibility that he might have been wrong. He envied Mikey climbing Janq'u Uma – he had dreamt about doing it while he was in Peru, but just never got around to it.

Mikey told them of his nervousness at the thought of meeting everyone at the funeral. What would they be expecting? How would they react to him talking normally? What should he say?

Strangely enough, Fr. O'Donnell told him, his experience was unknown in the town. His parents were nervous about telling anyone what was happening, for fear it mightn't end well. They wanted to wait until he was safely back home. When asked by friends and neighbours where he was, that they hadn't seen him around recently, they just said he had gone to stay for a while with a cousin up the country, helping out on their farm. The result was that nobody would expect him to be able to communicate any differently than they had known.

"'Just be yourself,' Fr. O'Donnell said. 'Take it as it comes. If people pass on without showing any expectation of a reply from you, accept it. You will know yourself when you should engage in conversation'. That gave me some comfort, but still the worries and anxieties were there.

"Fr. O'Donnell invited me to stay at the parochial house, which would be more comfortable than a cold, empty house and I wouldn't have to worry about shopping or cooking for myself. Not that I had any notion how to cook back then.

"There was a huge crowd at both the removal and funeral, a great send-off for Mamma and Dadda. At the removal, everyone filed by, shook my hand saying something like *'I'm sorry for your loss'*. Nobody dallied to say anything more because they had no expectation that I would understand. It was so easy just to nod and not say anything in reply to anyone. They just moved on. It was much the same at the funeral mass next day. Back then you will recall there was no question of a family member delivering a eulogy from the alter.

"Later at the cemetery there was torrential rain and Fr. O'Donnell flew through the prayers. People came up to me to express sympathy, to shake my hand, but with the awful weather there was no attempt to engage. They just wanted to get home and into dry clothes.

"I stood there feeling guilty, despite what Fr. O'Donnell had said. At the removal instead of just allowing everyone to hurry past, I should have spoken and told them how much I owed Mamma and Dadda. They deserved nothing less and I had failed in that simple task. What would people think when they discovered I could now communicate? And that I hadn't acknowledged the great debt I owed my parents? But those moments had passed.

"The last person at the graveside was Mrs. Dillon from two doors down. You'll remember Frank, I mentioned it was to her house Dadda had gone to phone Fr. O'Donnell that day Acahuana came home with me, and it was her house I phoned to talk to Mamma and Dadda after the operation. Well, I must say that day of the funeral, elderly and frail as she was, no amount of rain or any other weather was going to get in HER way. There she was in her mac, sou'wester and galoshes, waiting till everyone else had said their few words before coming up to me.

"She offered her sympathy before continuing: *'Well now Mikey O'Connor, you must tell me how that operation went down in South America'* I was stunned, but at the same time really happy that she knew and had started the conversation. Now perhaps I could redeem myself a little. *'It was magnificent,'* I replied, *'nothing short of a miracle for me. But we're wet enough as it is. I'll ask Fr. O'Donnell to drop us home and we can talk there in more comfort.'* She said better go to her house where we could have a cup of tea, there wouldn't be anything in Mamma and Dadda's house."

It seems after Mikey spoke with his parents from Lake Titicaca, they were so delighted they shared the news with Mrs. Dillon there and then, but they asked her not to say anything until he got back.

"She was amazed at the circumstances that led to my going to Lake Titacaca. *'But it wasn't so surprising when I thought about it. Your Mamma and Dadda were wonderful people. They would have done anything for you. It's just so tragic that they didn't live to see you come home, to hear your voice again, to hear all about how you got on over there. But at least they did have that phone call. You should have seen them afterwards. They were ecstatic. They were in heaven!'*

"She was interested in everything: *'What was Miami like? I'd love to have gone to Americay.'* When I told her about stopping in Iquitos: *'Well my God, you were in the middle of the jungle? What was it like? Did you see any monkeys or snakes or parrots?'* And later about the Altiplano and the Incas: *'Is that where the spuds came from? I heard someone once say there were no potatoes in this part of the world until Walter Raleigh brought them back from Peru. Is that true Mikey?'* When I told her about climbing Janq'u Uma she retorted: *'Well Mikey O'Connor you're a great mountaineer too! There'll be no stopping you now.'*

"Her final words to me were: *'Now Mikey make sure to live your life as a tribute to your Mamma and Dadda. They deserve nothing less. And make no mistake, I'll be watching you, and if you don't do right by them,*

I'll be back to haunt you!'

"That cup of tea and chat with Mrs. Dillon went some small way towards easing my guilt. Of course she spread the news about me, but strangely enough few seemed to want to believe her. *'Such an outlandish story couldn't possibly be true,'* they said. *'Maybe she's going a bit senile,'* they mused to one-another. *'I was at the funeral and saw no indication that Mikey had anything to say for himself,'* they replied. I heard all this from Fr. O'Donnell.

"Afterwards I went to stay with Fr. Bergin in Maynooth where he was professor of ethics at the seminary. At that time you will remember Maynooth University was mostly a seminary with few enough lay students. No shortage of young men for the priesthood back then. He arranged for me to have private classes so that I could have a chance to develop a career for myself."

Mikey was tired and we called it a day. His story turned over and over in my mind that night.

Did he go on to study at University? Did he return home afterwards to tell his story to friends and neighbours? How did they react? Where had he spent his life? What did he do? Did he marry and have a family?

There were so many questions I wanted to ask this man who had been a mere nineteen years old when all this happened. With so much on my mind I was tossing and turning for an age that night before I eventually managed to get to sleep.

VII

But sadly we never did talk again. When I came down for breakfast next morning, the matron approached me: "Frank," she said, "I'm afraid I have some very sad news. During the night Mikey suffered a massive stroke, and died a short time later. I noticed you talking to him a lot since you came here. You must have been very close friends. Please accept my deepest sympathy."

You could have knocked me over with a feather. Like myself, he was no spring chicken, yet he seemed healthy enough. Certainly it never occurred to me that his time might come so quickly. There was so much more I wanted to talk to him about.

The matron went on to say that as he had no close relatives to organise a funeral, there would be a short memorial service for him at the nursing home before burial at a nearby cemetery. In circumstances such as this, they would normally ask a resident friend to say a few words about the deceased. Since I seemed to have been the person to whom he was closest, would I do the honour? Of course I said yes.

The following day, a young priest came in to celebrate a funeral mass. Afterwards he asked me to come forward. I looked around. I really hadn't got to know more than a few of the other residents in the short time since I arrived. I saw many interested faces as well as the many expressionless faces of people who no longer had any energy for life. This I suppose is a reflection of the inevitable decline which awaits us all.

But I was there to honour Mikey.

> *"It is with great sadness that I heard Mikey O'Connor passed away the night before last. I first knew him eighty years ago when we sat side by side in class. All through his early years he seemed incapable of learning. There was no special education back then, but the nuns were dedicated and did their best. And he was a very genial companion, well liked despite his disability*

"But there was the inward Mikey known only to himself - bright, intelligent, willing to learn. And there it might well have remained for the rest of his life if he hadn't stopped in the street to dance a jig to the music of the pan-pipes. The players were from the Andes in South America. One of them, Acahuana, saw his inability to communicate, and told of the ancient knowledge of his people which enabled them to treat his condition, which they labelled 'severe communication disorder'.

"Mikey's parents, helped by two former missionaries to Peru, Fathers O'Donnell and Bergin, put great and blind trust in Acahuana. They allowed their son, Mikey, to go with this young man, and it proved they were right to do so. After treatment, Mikey could now communicate fluently in the manner all of you here who have spoken with him will know. But sadly, Mikey never saw his parents again, they had died in a tragic accident before he got back to Ireland.

"Of Mikey's later life I know absolutely nothing. I hadn't seen him for over sixty years until I came here recently. But this I do know: we must be very careful when making lazy, thoughtless decisions about people, like concluding that Mikey was a bit stupid, a no-hoper. How wrong we were back then, all of us who thought so."

I turned to the open coffin and said:

"Mikey, it was a pleasure to know you again after all those years."

I took up the book he had been reading when I arrived: *El Sueño del Celto* by the Peruvian author Mario Vargas Llosa. The Dream of the Celt. Very apposite, I thought, even if the book was about someone else[1]. He had been reading it in the Spanish original. I laid it in the coffin beside him before finishing:

"Rest in Peace, Mikey"

---

[1] A biography of Roger Casement.

The Reluctant Informer

I

By 1941 the war raging across Europe had brought the supply of petroleum products to a trickle in Ireland. Cars were effectively off the road. Only those with a special need to have a car could get a permit to enable them to buy petrol. There just wasn't enough to go around.

Mr. K lived up the mountain road and just like everyone else, his motor car was out of action for want of petrol. Like everyone else, to get around he walked or cycled. Only a month ago he himself, together with it seemed half the population of Clonmel, had cycled the fifty miles to Limerick and back to see Tipperary beat Cork in that most unusual Munster Hurling Final[1]. Everyone was in high spirits and no one complained about having to cycle.

However, his neighbour Mr. H who lived further up the hill seemed to have access to petrol, because he saw him driving past every so often. That man had no conscience, he thought. And as for the Guards, why were they permitting this breach of rationing regulations? Surely they knew but clearly they were doing nothing. Every time he saw Mr. H driving past, he got more and more incensed. He should really go to the Guards and put it up to them to do something about it.

But there was a problem. Would he be seen as an informer? He didn't see why, but he was very conscious of the disgust and disdain for the informer in the Irish psyche after the struggle for independence. He dithered.

But then he thought alerting the Guards to the situation would be nothing other than doing his civic duty, even if, as he felt sure, they

---

[1] Due to a foot and mouth outbreak in summer 1941, the Tipp team couldn't leave the county. Cork won the All-Ireland, but in October Tipp played Cork in a belated Munster Final, which Tipp won.

knew about it anyhow. Alerting the Guards was a matter of wanting the law to be upheld in his own country, which was rather different than going off telling tales to the security force of an occupying power. Still, for a long time he just couldn't do it.

But one more day when he spotted Mr. H driving, something inside snapped and he marched into town to the Guards Barracks. On the way he convinced himself that they would appreciate that he was doing his civic duty, have a quiet word with Mr. H, and there the matter would end.

Inside, Garda Malone was on desk duty. Mr. K reported what was going on, however he didn't receive the support he expected. Fifteen minutes later he stormed out.

II

At that very moment Sergeant O'Hara was walking into the Barracks and saw Mr. K striding out at a furious pace, with a face as black as thunder. Inside, Garda Malone was chuckling away to himself with a grin as broad as the ocean. On seeing the sergeant, he stood up straight and tried to look serious, but without success. When he eventually calmed down, the sergeant spoke.

"What's been going on here, Malone?" he asked in a rather stern voice. "I just saw Mr. K leaving with a face on him that would stop a clock. And here I find you looking as if the funniest thing ever had just happened. Explanation please."

While he was waiting for Malone to reply, he looked at the desk diary, but there was no entry. "And no entry either, I see," O'Hara added, "most irregular."

"Mr. K came in to report an incident, Sergeant."

"Well, why are the details not recorded? What's going on here?"

Malone replied: "It was about Mr. H from up the mountain road, Sergeant. We all know that he seems to have stored some petrol which he uses sparingly. He freewheels down to town once every few weeks, parks his car, does his business and starts the engine to drive the few miles back up the hill. Not sure he's fully respecting the law, but at his age and him shaky enough on the pins, he might never get back home again without the car."

"Yes, yes, we know all about this. But what's that got to do with Mr. K's visit here this morning?"

"Well that's the thing, Sarge. Mr. K is incensed that with everyone reduced to cycling or walking, Mr. H can continue driving without as much as a whisper from the Force. He came in here to complain about this carry-on and demanded that we do something about it."

"What does he want us to do? Throw the auld geezer in jail? You, me and the rest of the Force have better things to be doing."

"Well you know that Sarge, and all the rest of us do, but Mr. K doesn't agree. I listened to him while he was giving me the story, which of course we already knew. I didn't write anything down because I suspected you wouldn't want me to put us in a position where we had to open a case file. He kept telling me to write it down, but I waited until he was finished. Then, sez I to him:

"'So, Mr. K, you're coming in here to inform on Mr. H, is that it?'

"Well he nearly hit the roof. The very suggestion that our Mr. K might be branded an informer put paid to his complaint and he stormed out."

At this, Garda Malone started his chuckling again. Sergeant O'Hara, couldn't resist and joined in. Just then, the Sergeant happened to be looking out the window and spotted the Superintendent coming back. He immediately signalled to Garda Malone to shape up, which he did. Both managed to calm down just in time.

As Superintendent McCarthy walked in, there wasn't a squeak or a giggle out of the pair. The Sergeant was saying: "Well done, Garda Malone," then immediately saluted the Super who said: "That's what I like to see, good work being acknowledged," as he disappeared into his office.

III

Mr. K stormed home like a demon. People turned their heads as he passed. *"What's got into him?"* they asked themselves. When he got in home, he slammed the front door and slumped into a chair. He was close to tears.

Eventually, he calmed down and reflected on what had happened. Instead of having the quiet satisfaction of doing his civic duty, he had been branded an informer. He couldn't imagine anything worse. Those bastards in the Garda Barracks would now be having a laugh among themselves. And unlike the police force of an occupying power who would guard their informants well, they would have no compunction about spreading the story to all and sundry.

His reputation would be ruined. And not only that, Mr. H would continue driving up the road, a constant reminder of his foolhardy desire to carry out his civic duty. He would rue this day forever.

The Secret of Killamery

Celtic High Cross at Killamery

The Hi-B

All this started with a chance conversation in the Hi-B, a pub on Oliver Plunkett St. in Cork. It was August 2009. I had arranged to meet a friend I hadn't seen for three years. Or so I thought.

While savouring with anticipation the rising head on my first pint of Beamish in three years, I was brought back to reality with a jolt when the barman answered the phone, turned to me, and asked whether I was Jimmy Sheehy. I said yes, not that there were too many other candidates in the bar. It could only be Johnny, no one else knew I would be there. I hadn't got around to getting a phone since my return, so we were relying on the old fashioned way of contacting someone you were supposed to meet: phone the barman. Something had turned up and Johnny would be unable to join me.

I paid for my pint, sat down, and took a look around. The place hadn't changed one iota. The same furniture, a ban on mobile phones. There was a couple in the corner. And me. That was the extent of the clientele at about 7 o'clock that evening. I intended to sip my drink slowly, go back home and see what was on the box.

But circumstances intervened which were to lead to the most amazing, not to say barely credible experience imaginable. But credible or not, it happened. Please bear with me.

A guy came in looking a bit the worse for wear, went to the bar and ordered a drink. He wore an old well-worn leather jacket, denim shirt, jeans and desert boots. I thought desert boots belonged to the past, but clearly not.

Then, pint of Guinness in hand, he looked around, walked over in my direction and sat down beside me. He plonked his drink on the table and started, "D'you mind if I sit down here?" Definitely a Dub, by his accent. "No, you're fine," I replied, not wanting to refuse as he was already sitting down. After exchanging a few pleasantries, in the course of which we also exchanged names – he was Luke – I mentioned I was just back from Central America.

"Really?" he said. "Must have been an interesting trip. I've been reading a lot recently about the Aztecs and the Mayas. Some people! They seem to have had some secret knowledge about the Universe. You know, like all that current talk about multiple universes. I think they found out how to travel from one universe to another. And back. That's where all the knowledge came from to build their civilisations. Also that mysterious crowd who inhabited Teotihuacán ages before the King of Spain sent out his Conquistadores (which he pronounced slowly and deliberately Cong-kiss-tah-doors)".

"Wow!" I thought to myself, "quite a lot to take in all at once". But I said nothing for a moment. Then I started: "Teotihuacán is quite a fascinating place. It's not far from Mexico City but it's a world apart. I was there. I found myself in this vast site with an avenue straight down the middle – Avenida de los Muertos, the Avenue of the Dead. Must be over a mile long. Right at the end is the pyramid of the Moon and about half way down on your right is the enormous pyramid of the Sun. And there are many more magnificent buildings on either side. Seems their civilisation was at its peak a thousand years before the Spanish arrived. But I didn't hear anyone talking about multiple universes".

This multiple universe thing and the idea that we could travel from one world to the next is just drink talking, I said to myself. But, as I had nothing much else on the cards that evening, I decided to encourage him. Definitely a better bet than struggling to find something worth watching on the box. "But tell me about this multiple universe theory Luke," I continued.

However, instead of multiple universes, he started talking about Latin America. "Fascinating place Teotihuacán, I'd love to go there.

Funny this Latin America connection. Myself, I'm just back from Peru. I was three years in Mali and when I returned I decided a trip to Peru was just what I needed. It could just as well have been Mexico: Peru and Mexico were both on my radar. It's amazing that all these civilisations were thriving in that part of the world while the Greeks and the Romans and God knows who else here in Europe thought they were the centre of everything. I got to see the old mud-walled city of Chan Chan in the North, the Nazca lines in the South and Machu Picchu up in the mountains. Like Teotihuacán, Chan-Chan flourished long before the Spanish arrived – it's the largest mud-walled city ever built. But they had been conquered by the Inca before Columbus set sail. And Machu Picchu was never found by the Spaniards. As for the Nazca lines, impressive and all as they are no one has a clue as to what they were about.

"But back to all these Universes. It's the Many Worlds theory, actually. But I suppose that's just language. Either way, it amounts to the same thing".

He soon got into his stride. "Cosmologists have been trying to develop equations to describe everything. As well as the Many Worlds theory, they have come up with this thing called String Theory. It seems there's no substance to anything. It's all waves and God knows what. I mean, I could give you a poke, I'd feel the resistance of your body and you'd feel the poke."

I put my hands up and sat back an inch or two. I had no interest in receiving a poke from this boyo.

"Take it easy," he responded, "I'm not going to poke you, this was just by way of explaining that we all think we and the world are made of stuff that you can touch and feel. But this string theory, let me tell you, that's something else altogether. There's no substance to anything. Everything is a series of vibrations. I can't get my head around what exactly is vibrating, but that, my friend, has serious implications."

He may have been a bit under the weather, but as he got into his stride, he exuded confidence and certainty about what he was saying. He continued:

"Because when they started analysing the mathematical formulae about all these strings, they discovered that it leads to lots of dimensions in the world we live in and the existence of lots of universes. In fact, an infinity of universes, if you can get your head around that, my friend!"

I couldn't get a word in edgewise to explain my difficulty in *getting my head around that, my friend!'*. He was on a roll.

"As regards Teotihuacán, there really is no evidence, just a notion of mine. But before I get going about Killamery, let me just explain a few things."

"Killamery?" I spluttered out while trying to take a slug from my pint. "I'm afraid you've lost me now. Hard enough to get my head around this Many Worlds thing, and now you're lumping in Teotihuacán and Killamery—wherever that might be. And what in the name of God might these places have to do with Many Worlds?"

He didn't respond, just took a slug from his own pint before continuing.

"All of these Many Worlds could be anywhere, even right here. In Ireland. In the Hi-B here in Cork. There's no reason why not. You see, if you're only a series of vibrations, then there's no reason why someone else – what did you say your name was?" "Jimmy." "Well Jimmy, there could be another Jimmy occupying exactly the same space as you, but you would never know because the vibrations are out of phase. You're just back from Mexico or someplace, right?"

"Yes."

"Well you had to make a decision to return to Ireland. I mean, you could have decided to stay on in Mexico or Guatemala or wherever."

"I suppose. I actually did consider staying in Mexico, but decided to come home."

"There you go, see? In another Universe you are in Mexico and you wouldn't be sitting here next to me drinking a pint. By the way while we're on the subject of pints, I'm sure you'll have another."

I just about had time to say mine would be a Beamish before he ordered two more pints. I didn't object, I was starting to get interested in this Many Worlds thing. He came back from the bar, plonked the pints on the table in front of us and reverted to his theories.

"The question is, could we travel to all these Worlds? And back?"

"Hold on there, a sec," I said. "A few minutes ago we were just talking about the possibility of there being other Worlds, and now suddenly you're wondering if we could get to one? That's a big step. Let's suppose we could, sure I might be stranded in a world full of dinosaurs. What would I do then? Not sure I'd last too long there, not that I'd want to anyway."

"Fair point, my friend, fair point. But you see, if I'm understanding all this correctly, you can't just travel to any old world. It would have to be one where you have a presence. You know, a place where you made a decision to go or to leave. So it's like this: you were in Mexico and you thought about coming back to Ireland, and you did – otherwise we wouldn't be here slugging down pints together, now would we?

"My theory, for what it's worth, is that you can only travel to another world where you have a presence, so Mexico would be an obvious choice for you. I, on the other hand, might be able to make Peru, seeing as I just came back from there. Now those Nazca lines might just be the sort of place that had inter-worlds technology transfer. That Swiss guy Erich von Däniken was onto the general idea, but he said it was all to do with visits by gods or astronauts. Gods, I'm afraid, are not my thing."

I interrupted: "Luke, this is all very interesting. I'll indulge your theory for the moment. Now, tell me what EXACTLY you think would happen if I did cross to another world?"

He sat back again for a few moments before replying. "There's no consensus on that, not even consensus as to whether it could happen," he replied. "But here's my theory. It's a funny thing, but I don't believe you would disappear from this world. You'd still be here, living your ordinary 'this world' life. But your mind, brain, whatever, would duplicate and meld into 'your mind' in the other Universe."

"Hmm. So let's suppose I 'meld' into my alter ego in Mexico, then I can still go about my normal life here? And will I then also know about what's happening in Mexico?"

"It's not like that," he said as he sat back, in deep thought again it seemed. Probably about how he could explain things to me. After a few minutes he continued.

"You're here in Ireland, sitting down in the Hi-B having a pint with me. You know all about your life in Mexico or Central America up to the point where you made a decision to return to Ireland rather than stay in Mexico. Your world split from that moment, leading to two parallel life experiences for Jimmy: one here, drinking a pint with me; and the other where you continued living in Mexico and about which you at this time know ab-so-lute-ly nothing! Zero! Zilch! But that there is this other life experience of Jimmy in a parallel world is not in doubt. At least not by me."

"But if I could find some way to get across to that other world..." I started, but Luke put up his hand and stopped me in my tracks.

"Jimmy, Jimmy my friend, I'll try again. But just one thing—no questions or interruptions until I'm finished. OK?" All this as he made a show of finishing off his pint.

I got the (not so subtle) hint. "I suppose you'd manage another one of those? Guinness, is it?" I asked. "Thank you my friend, I would indeed," he replied. When I returned, I sat back and folded my arms. "OK, Luke, I'm listening."

"So let's take this step by step. You made a choice to return from Mexico—which you had the option of not making. If my understanding is correct, then at the moment of that decision, a quantum event was precipitated, which split your universe in two.

"It would be a bit like coming to a fork in a road. You have to decide which road to take: Ireland or Mexico? Only with the quantum event you take both. At the same time. From that moment on there were two Jimmys, living in two distinct worlds. One of those brought you here to the Hi-B, and the other – well, who knows where that Jimmy is now or what he is doing off out in Mexico, that is if he hasn't moved on somewhere else. He might even be back in Ireland. But remember, these are not the Mexico or Ireland that we know, rather a parallel Mexico or Ireland in a parallel world. Unless we can find some way to reconnect the two lives, each will go their own separate way. So far so good, nothing complicated. Right?"

Not quite so far so good, I thought to myself, there's the not so small matter of accepting that there's another me in a parallel world across some parallel Atlantic Ocean in some parallel Mexico. And what about this *'quantum event'*? Where did this come from? Mind boggling to put it mildly. But I had agreed no interruptions, so I just said "Right!"

"Let's just assume for now that we can find a way to transfer your brain, your consciousness, whatever, to that other world and meld it into that other-world Mexican you. Let's leave the details to one side for now and just go with the theory."

"OK," I mumbled.

"The next thing is to try and understand what might happen when your consciousness crosses the barrier from our world here in the Hi-B and enters the consciousness of Jimmy Mexico—how do you like that name, Jimmy Mexico?—in that other world."

I said nothing and he continued. "The first thing we can assume is that of course this transfer of consciousness does not leave behind a mindless Jimmy here in this world.

"I suppose it would be a bit like backing up your laptop hard drive: there would be two identical copies, but each copy could be edited separately, leading in time to two quite different sets of contents. At the moment of transfer, you here in the Hi-B, or wherever you happened to be, wouldn't necessarily know what had happened, apart perhaps from some fleeting feeling or sensation about Mexico.

"So now the transfer has happened. From that moment on, the Mexican other world Jimmy becomes fully aware of everything in the experience of Jimmy back here in Ireland. From the moment you decided to leave Mexico right up to the moment of the transfer. Including the fact that we sat here in the Hi-B discussing the very possibility of the transfer. So he will know whether the option of staying in Mexico was or wasn't the better option. And of course he also knows how his life turned out in Mexico, because he was there all the time. I imagine he would find that rather strange and daunting. He might think it was a dream, however, dreams tend to fade away when you wake up, but this wouldn't. I wonder how he'd deal with it? Would he be afraid to tell anyone lest they question his sanity? I don't know. I hope you are following all this." I nodded to assure him I was.

He continued: "The two parallel lives—one in Ireland in our world, the other in Mexico in that parallel world would each continue on their own trajectory. You here in Ireland would no more know what was going on in Mexico than you do now, while that other world Mexican guy would know nothing about what was happening back in Ireland after the transfer. That might be the end of it. Unless there was a repatriation of your consciousness." He stayed quiet for a moment, again just gazing into space.

His logic was impeccable and I understood how it might work. In theory. But still I was having a hard time getting my head around the possible reality of all this. "Repatriation?" I interjected. "You're making sense logically, but that doesn't mean it's easy to keep up with you. You better explain this repatriation."

He didn't reply immediately and I also remained silent. After a few moments he continued. "This might never happen. But let's just say there was a repatriation of the copy of you that went to Mexico, back to its rightful home. Back inside your brain.

"Let's suppose that months or years later, or any time after the transfer, the copy of your brain that went to Mexico manages to transfer back to Ireland. BECAUSE that copy had spent some time melded into Jimmy Mexico, YOU here in Ireland will now know what your experience would have been if you had stayed on there, up to that moment of repatriation. God only knows what you would think if and when this happened. Maybe you would wish you had stayed out there, or maybe you would be glad you came home. It would be just the same for you as it was for the guy in Mexico when you landed in on top of him. Would it now be your turn to question your own sanity? Could you talk to someone about it without provoking raised eyebrows and whispering behind your back?

"I'm not sure that Mexican guy would even know the repatriation had happened. I mean, at the first transfer he had suffered the trauma or whatever of suddenly finding in his memory all about how his life would have turned out if he had returned to Ireland, but only up to that moment. There would have been no further information about life in Ireland after that point.

"I hope all that is a bit clearer than mud," he said with a big grin on his face. "Repatriation. I like that word, I think it fits the circumstance."

He sat back and looked up at the ceiling, seemingly deep in thought. I was still trying to fathom it all out when he continued.

"So that would be the state of affairs, OR, as your man Spooner would have said 'the fate of a stairs'." He chuckled to himself before proceeding, somewhat off the point of worlds. "You remember back in '66, the IRA or someone blew up Nelson's Pillar in Dublin? Well, my Da must have bought every edition of the Dublin Opinion because there were stacks of them in the spare bedroom. I was going through some of them once when I came across the edition after the Pillar was blown up. There was a photograph of the stump of the Pillar on the front cover with the caption 'A Terrible Fate of a Stairs'. Some genius must have dreamt it up after a few pints."

He reverted to the topic of worlds: "But I digress. You would now have to deal with all this, just like he had to. Except you would have one BIG advantage."

He sat back again, taking a slug from his pint, which gave me time to let all this sink in. I didn't know what to think. I was torn between writing it all off as drink talk and being intrigued with the possibility of inter-world travel.

"What advantage is that?" I asked.

"You, my friend, could come and talk to me. And of course *vice-versa*."

Now, we both sat back. I remained deep in thought for several minutes before saying anything. And in fairness to Luke, he allowed me the space to mull over everything he said.

Then: "You know, Luke, you have explained everything very clearly, no ambiguity at all. I would even say it all makes logical sense, except for one thing: is any of this based on hard facts? Is it based on reality? Is there even the remotest possibility that you or I or anyone else could actually experience this? Are the scientists, cosmologists, etc agreed on this string theory? What are these quantum events? Where are all these other worlds? Or is it all pie in the sky? Some sort of science fiction? Nothing more than an exercise in logic, perhaps?"

For the first time his certainty seemed to falter. "That's the thing," he said. "The scientific community is divided on all this. And as for the possibility of travel between universes, there is little if any support for this. In fact the general consensus is that it is not possible. That's why you have to look to somewhere other than science." He was staring into space, wondering perhaps whether I would end up questioning his sanity. And I was having my doubts, it must be said.

Then he continued. "You asked me what Killamery might have to do with all this. Actually everything. But the hour is late, and I'm not sure that me continuing to talk at this stage will do either of us much good. If you are genuinely interested in pursuing this, we could take a trip to Killamery tomorrow. It's on the road between Clonmel and Kilkenny. We could take the 11.20 bus to Kilkenny in the morning, that would get us there. Are you on?"

I wondered what I was getting into. But I have to admit I was intrigued and wanted to find out where all this would lead. In any case, what else would I be doing? I had been offered a job in Galway which wasn't due to start for a month. I might as well do this as hang around being bored. So I said, "Yes, see you at the bus station in the morning." And with that we shook hands, and went our separate ways.

I was staying with my parents while waiting to move to Galway, which I planned to do as soon as I could arrange a place of my own there. When I got home, Ma and Da were just heading upstairs to bed. Da said "Goodnight Jimmy. Don't forget to lock the front door and turn off the lights before you turn in." I replied "Don't worry, I won't forget." Then I continued: "Ma, be sure to wake me up early in the morning, I've promised to meet a guy at the bus station at about ten past eleven."

Ma turned around and said, "Now where are you off to? It wouldn't by any chance be a young lady you're meeting?"

"Ah no, Ma, nothing like that. 'Night Da, 'night Ma."

I went to the kitchen, made a cup of coffee, cut a slice of Ma's home-baked fruit cake and went into the living room. I selected a CD of Mozart's Eine Kleine Nachtmusik, sat back and relaxed in the tranquil atmosphere, sipping my cup of coffee, and going over and over and over what must surely have been my strangest encounter ever. And there have been a few strange ones, let me tell you.

For sure, Luke had laid out his case well and everything he posited made logical sense. But was it based on anything more than wild imagination and an exercise in logic? And what was all this about Killamery? The last movement of Eine Kleine Nachtmusik ended and I was too tired to start looking up Killamery, if indeed it warranted anything in any encyclopædia. I went to bed, and yes, I did remember to check the front door and turn off the lights.

It wasn't my best night's sleep ever, though I imagine the combination of too many pints and the late night coffee all contributed. But I did eventually nod off and when I awoke I was surprised to see it was already after nine. Time to get up, have a quick shower before breakfast, and head to the bus station.

When I got downstairs, Ma was in the kitchen. "Good morning, Jimmy. You look a bit rough this morning. Too much cavorting last night? And what about this guy you're meeting?"

"Just met him in the Hi-B last night. Johnny never turned up and I had a few pints with this guy, Luke. We're taking a trip to Killamery," I said. "Any chance of a boiled egg, Ma?"

"Sit down there and I'll wet the tea, put on some toast and boil an egg. But tell me, where's Killamery and what's there? Are you sure you're not keeping something from me? Some nice young girl you also happened to meet last night?"

"Ah no, Ma. I told you last night, nothing like that. Just that Luke thinks there's something interesting there he'd like to show me. And since I've nothing much else to do, I might as well go."

"Nothing much to do? What about painting the back room like you promised?"

"Ah Ma, of course I'll paint the back room, but not this week. Next week definitely!"

"You said that last week and I'm still waiting. And tell me, where is Killamery? Can't say I ever heard of it. Will you be back tonight?"

"Somewhere between Clonmel and Kilkenny. I don't know, I suppose we'll be back tonight. Depends on bus times. Luke didn't say anything about staying away."

Killamery

I was at the bus station just after eleven and a few minutes later Luke wandered in. On the bus, I didn't launch into a continuation of our discussions in the Hi-B. I wasn't ready for more of that, I just wanted to see how the day would turn out. Instead, I asked Luke about himself. I knew nothing about who he was apart from our strange conversation the night before.

We were of a similar age, both in our mid 30s. He was just a year older than me. Turns out he went to University to study physics, which is where he became interested in cosmology. However he flunked his third year exams, and instead of doing repeats, he left studying behind. He trained as a controls & instrument technician and worked on the Intel Fab building up in County Kildare for a few years. He really enjoyed being on site, it suited him much better than academia. And he was hopeful of getting a job in Intel again. But just because he left academia was not to say that he dropped his interest in cosmology and quantum mechanics – clearly he didn't.

"You know Jimmy," he said, "you need a degree to get past the recruitment people, but not to pursue your passion. I reckon my personal studies have taken me to a level of knowledge and understanding above and beyond many academics. But of course they'll never acknowledge that because I'm missing the piece of paper. But I couldn't care less. They're constrained in their Ivory Towers whereas I'm a free spirit."

He then went on to talk about the previous three years of his life. He had seen an advert looking for volunteers to help small communities in West Africa set up local power supplies based on solar cells. While he knew little enough about this, his background was just the thing for the project. He was interviewed, accepted as a volunteer and posted to a small village near Bamako in the southwest of Mali, and some thousand kilometres from the mystical city of Timbuktu. During his time there he installed a number of small solar cell power systems, backed up by batteries. He worked with locals and trained them in installation and maintenance.

I asked if he had had an opportunity to visit Timbuktu – one of my memories from growing up was hearing the phrase 'he's gone to Timbuktu' to signal that someone was gone away somewhere, but you weren't being told where. Neither, I must say, did we back then have any idea where Timbuktu was, or even if it was a real place.

"About six months before I left," he replied, "a local man Ibrahim, who was a bit of a wheeler dealer, asked me if I'd go with him to Timbuktu. He had gotten a contract to deliver some solar cells and batteries to Timbuktu and decided I was just the man to go with him to ensure the people up there knew what they were doing. I was delighted to have the opportunity to go there, something I had planned to do before I left Mali. This was a chance to go there with free transport. I checked with the volunteer agency if it would be OK to head off for a week or so. As it involved the very thing for which I had volunteered, they said no problem.

"I talked last night about the wonders of Peru, but I can tell you Timbuktu is also quite a place. We in Europe, in Ireland, have no concept of the wealth of history, culture, art, architecture of Africa. We were always taught that they depended on our missionaries to be educated, to bring them into the modern world. I'm not saying that there weren't very dedicated missionaries who did excellent work, but we learned nothing about the history or culture of Africa. It was as if such didn't exist and it needed Europeans to educate them and drag them out of their primitive and ignorant ways. Nothing could be further from the truth.

"I don't think any Europeans had even seen Timbuktu before sometime in the 1800s. But between the 1300s and 1600s it flourished. It was a thriving centre of a vast kingdom covering much of West Africa, as big as Western Europe, I believe. It was a major centre of learning and culture. I tell you, Jimmy we were given a very jaundiced viewpoint."

Quite a lot to take in. I had to admit that I knew almost nothing about Africa. But at one level that wasn't really a surprise. Our history of the world was very much based on Western Europe and North America. I told him that he mirrored to some extent my recent past.

"I too was a volunteer abroad—in Guatemala. And just like yourself in Mali, I knew hardly anything about Guatemala before going there. There was just this big blob called Latin America which the Spanish and Portuguese had conquered, and little else. I had to be there to learn about the Mayan culture.

"I was working to set up a local agricultural co-operative near Chichicastenango in the western highlands. A thoroughly beautiful place in the rugged mountains, really lovely people, beautifully colourful local handmade clothing, craft markets, you name it. Contrary to what you might think, they don't all speak Spanish. Mostly they speak the local language, K'iche' with a smattering of Spanish. I studied Spanish and speak it passably well, but I never managed more than a few words of K'iche'.

"That was the easy part of working there. I can tell you it is not an easy task to try and organise campesinos into co-operatives in a country with the elite's fanatical hatred of anything which might strengthen and give some power to the rural dwellers."

"That must have been some experience," he replied, before continuing with his own story. "After Mali, I felt I needed something totally different before settling down in Ireland. So as I said last night, I headed off to Peru for a few months. Fascinating country. You know the capital, Lima, is in the Atacama Desert. It almost never rains. Sometimes the humidity can be stifling for weeks on end and you feel like there has to be a downpour to clear the air. But it never comes. Met a lovely lassie the time I went to Machu Picchu. Maria Inés. She was Chilean and we were walking the Inca Trail together. Thought about staying out in that part of the world and following her back to Chile, but I have to admit I didn't think she felt that strongly about me. In any case my brother was due to be married in Dublin and he had asked me to be Best Man. So that was that."

Just then, the bus pulled in to Clonmel. "Won't be long now," Luke said. Sure enough, twenty minutes later Luke requested a stop. We had arrived at Killamery.

The village of Killamery is little more than a cross roads. Not much to see. I imagine people drive past it without even realising that it is a village with a name. I asked Luke the inevitable question: "What are we doing at this cross roads in the middle of nowhere?"

"Let's take a short walk," he said. We turned off the main road and after a few hundred metres we came to an old graveyard with a very impressive looking Celtic High Cross in the middle and the remains of an old church in one corner. Then he started to explain.

"I hope you can indulge me for a few moments while I give you a bit of background about this place. It seems that St. Gobán and a host of monks left a settlement at Old Leighlin before a Church Synod in 633 AD. The Synod, by the way, was all about resolving a difference between Rome and Ireland as to when Easter Sunday should be celebrated. You might wonder how such trivial matters can cause serious disagreements, but that's another day's work.

"Anyway, these monks founded a new monastery here at Killamery. During Gobán's time the new monastery flourished. It seems there were as many as a thousand monks living there at its peak. There is a 9th - century book – 'The Martyrology of Oengus' - which records all this.

"The High Cross there in front of us is from sometime in the 8th century, but that old ruin of a Church over there to our left dates from much later."

So a bit of a historian as well as a cosmologist, I thought to myself. "All very interesting", I replied. "But typical Island of Saints and Scholars stuff. None of this gives me the remotest notion as to why we are here."

"Just be patient my friend, be patient" he continued. "Let's walk back to the village cross roads and give our custom to *The Mad Monk.*" Ten minutes later we were sitting down outside with a couple of pints of stout in front of us.

He continued talking about the monastery: "The monks there dedicated their life to prayer and the worship of God almighty. To feed themselves they tilled the land, kept goats and cattle, milked them and made butter and cheese. They would have been largely self-sufficient, but also well integrated with the surrounding communities with whom they would have traded some of their products. They needed to do this: they couldn't produce everything themselves. And before you say it, yes, this is the usual Island of Saints and Scholars stuff. But I think it's important to understand some background.

"One of the monks, *Fionán,* who perhaps came from some nearby settlement, is a really interesting character. This was in the early ninth century.

"Fionán, it seems, couldn't get his mind off a young lassie by the name of Bríd. He went off to live the life of a hermit for a while to see if he could rid himself of his obsession. And you know what happened next? He arrived back at the monastery with an amazing story, that he had seen another world where he had married that same lassie. Not the sort of story that was likely to be given any credence back then. Nor today either I imagine.

"In any case, he persisted with his story. The abbot declared he must have gone mad. This is all written down in the Annals of Killamery which are kept at the Monastic Archives Museum in Kilkenny.

"If I have whetted your interest, we should visit there tomorrow. I've spoken to the owner of this establishment. She also runs a bed and breakfast business and has a couple of rooms upstairs. They're ours for tonight if we wish. What do you say?"

What could I say? "Yes," I answered without delay, "I've come this far and it would be a shame to turn back now."

"Good," said Luke, "and just as well too. The last bus for Cork passed by half an hour ago."

The owner rustled up a nice meal for us, which we ate inside. There was a slight chill in the air by now. Afterwards we continued talking about this and that for a while, then around 9 o'clock a few local traditional musicians dropped in and entertained us for a couple of hours.

The next morning we came down to the aroma of a full Irish breakfast, which set us up for the day. There was a bus for Kilkenny due to pass by at 10.50 and we were on it.

The Archives

At the Monastic Archives, Luke requested permission to view the Annals of Killamery. There were formalities to go through, IDs to be presented, request for any mobile phones or other photographic devices to be handed over lest we try to take photographs of these old, delicate and priceless pages. Also there would be an archivist with us at all times and she alone would be allowed handle the documents while we could request sight of particular pages.

An index document listed the various pages and their contents. Luke asked to see the pages relating to the monk Fionán. We were taken to a viewing room with dim lighting and air conditioning to protect the ancient documents.

Twenty minutes later the archivist returned with a large document, bound in what appeared to be a fairly recently made leather cover. Apparently when the annals were discovered, they were just a collection of loose pages in a lead lined timber box. What was salvageable of the wood had been carbon dated and corresponded with the dates on a number of the annals, which essentially proved their authenticity.

The Annals date from the 700s to the 900s, the period when the monastery was at its peak. Many pages are frayed and worn, parts of some pages and indeed several entire pages seemed to be missing, victims of the ravages of time.

The archivist, wearing silk gloves and using a tweezers, went carefully through the document until she came to four pages, worn and frayed but reasonably intact, which she extracted for our perusal. On no account should we try to touch the pages.

"The incidents described in these pages seem exceptional.

Scholars have spent quite some time going over them, wondering how to interpret the apparent experience of a monk travelling to another world. Not to mention a certain bishop who recently tried to have them deemed an obvious fake," she said. She laid out the first page concerning certain events as reported by Fionán.

It was written in Latin. The archivist noted that back then the only punctuation used was to separate words and sentences, a practice introduced by the Irish monks to make manuscripts more legible. Centuries earlier this same practice had been introduced by the Greeks, but the Romans later dispensed with it. Punctuation as we know it was developed after the invention of the printing press. There was an English translation:

> *Fionán lived the life of a hermit for a time on Eninis. He returned saying that his soul had travelled to another world where he was married to Bríd, with whom he was in love before coming here. I was worried it was the work of Satan himself. I forbade him from speaking about it with anyone other than Brother Ultan.*
>
> *+Abbot Ciarán, Year of Our Lord 804.*

We asked the archivist about Eninis – had she any idea where that was? She explained that *Eninis*[1] was the Old Irish name for Great Saltee Island, long since obsolete. Saltee, it seems, comes from Old Norse *salt øy*, meaning salt island. Eninis suffered a Viking raid in 922[2], in which some 1,200 were slain, indicating there was probably a monastic settlement there at that time, although no records exist.

---

[1] See Journal Irish Archaeology, 2001, vol 10, pp 93-119; Prof. John Sheehan: *A Viking Age Maritime Haven: A Reassessment of the Island Settlement at Beginish, Co. Kerry.*

[2] Chronicon Scotorum Annal CS922.

Next to that page was another undated record, somewhat worn and tattered. It was a sketch seeming to show the way from Killamery to Eninis, with certain monasteries indicated, perhaps where a pilgrim could find lodgings along the way. It seems there is a lot of uncertainty surrounding locations of monasteries in the pre-Norman period. The places indicated were known monastic sites during Norman times It is suspected many such had a much older history.

The various monasteries indicated would provide lodgings along the way. The first leg took him to Ahenny, perhaps to visit his family. From there he would follow the Lingaun river, *Loinneán*, to a monastery at Fiddown, *Feach Dún*, on the banks of the Suir, *Abha na Siúire*; at Ballinlaw, *Baile an Ladha*, a ferry would take him across the Barrow, *an Bearú*. He would continue to Clonmine, *Cluain Mín*, with the final leg on land taking him to Inish, *Inis*, from where the monks, it would seem, would ferry him out to *Eninis*, Great Saltee Island.

Amazing, I thought to myself. I was becoming totally absorbed in this history of monastic times, of which I really had no more than the barest minimum knowledge. I was beginning to understand why Luke brought me here. But there was more. The next document was Fionán's own angry rebuttal of his silencing, again with translation provided:

> *Why do ye not believe that my soul travelled to another world? Do we not believe in an all-powerful God? He whom we honour? Who made the world in which we live? Who are you to deny that same God the power to create two or more worlds? You would rather forbid me from talking about this. But writing about it is not talking.*
>
> *Fionán, Year of Our Lord 819*

Fionán seemed to be in no doubt about the reality of what had happened. And there was no indication he was aware of Abbot

127

Ciarán's entry many years earlier, or if he was, he made no reference to it. There was also a fascinating poem on the page, written in Old Irish, - *Messe ocus Pangar Bán*[1]. Translation:

> *I and Pangur Bán my cat,*
> *'Tis a like task we are at:*
> *Hunting mice is his delight,*
> *Hunting words I sit all night.*
>
> *Oftentimes a mouse will stray*
> *In the hero Pangur's way;*
> *Oftentimes my keen thought set*
> *Takes a meaning in its net.*
>
> *So in peace our task we ply,*
> *Pangur Bán, my cat, and I;*
> *In our arts we find our bliss,*
> *I have mine and he has his.*

But this was not the end of it. Some years later there was an entry by another Abbot, Ultan, who wrote:

> *Why did Fionán write about his soul travelling to another world, despite promising not to talk about it? But we permit this to remain so that generations to come may understand why we considered him insane. May God have mercy on his soul.*
>
> *+Abbot Ultan, Year of Our Lord 822*

---

[1] *'I and Pangur Bán'* a 9th century poem by an unknown Irish monk at a monastery in Reichenau, in what is now modern day Germany. Translation by Robin Flower.

postquam

ꝼıonanus

commoratus ermeticus aliquantisper in Emne regressus priusquam huc venit dixit animam ad alium regnum measse ubi in matrimonio Dridam quam amabat habuerat · timui opus Satani fuisse · de eo eum dicere nisi adelpho Ultano votui ·

ab + Ciaranus
an Dom DCCCIV

Annal 804 AD : record #31

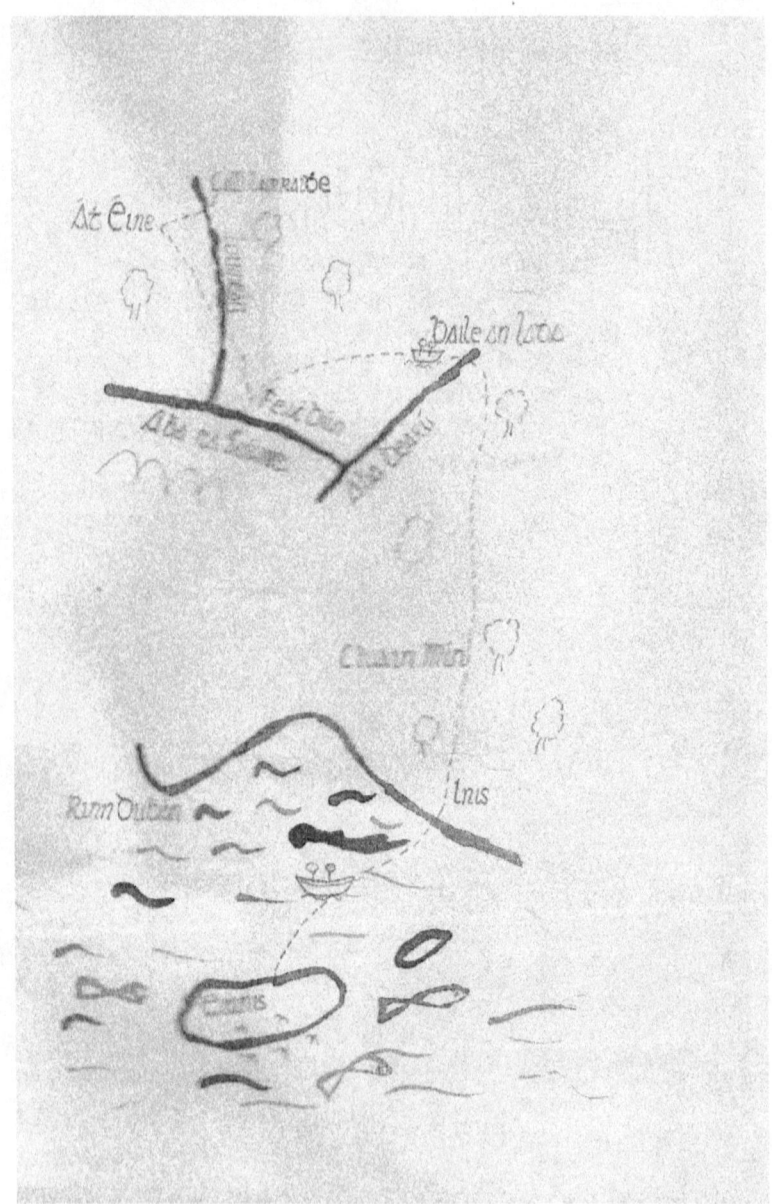

Undated record

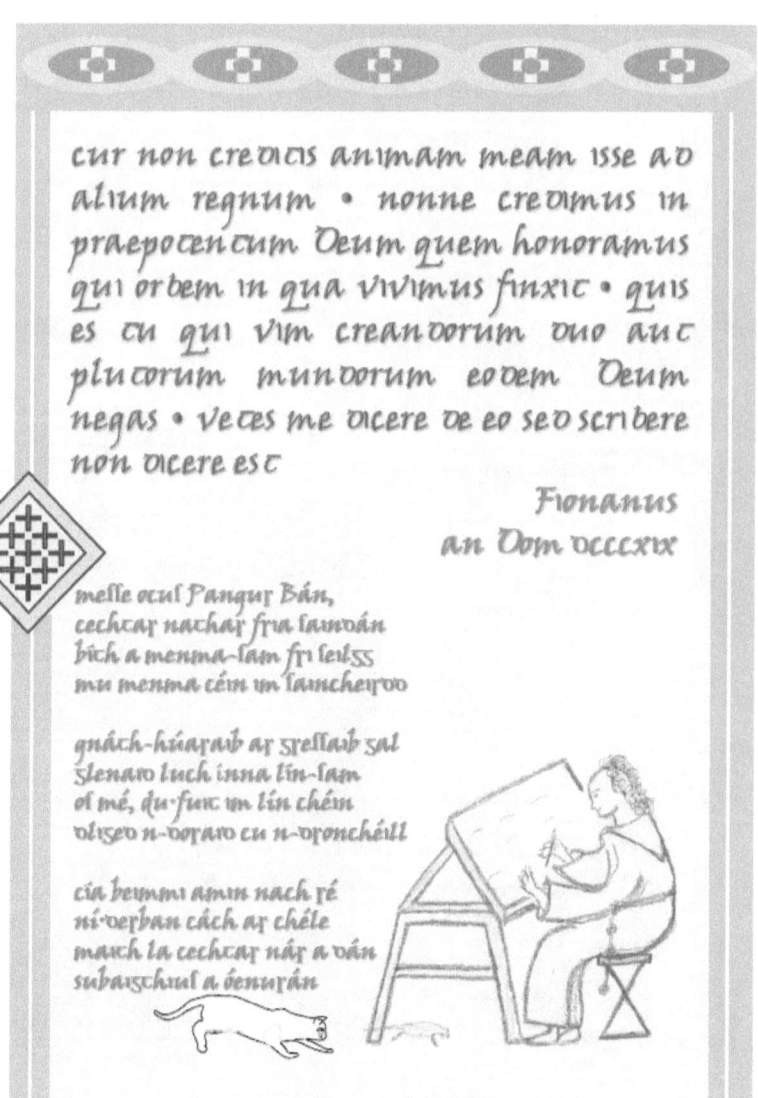

cur non creoicis animam meam isse ao
alium regnum • nonne creoimus in
praepocencum Oeum quem honoramus
qui orbem in qua vivimus finxic • quis
es cu qui vim creanoorum ouo auc
plucorum munoorum eooem Oeum
negas • veces me oicere oe eo seo scribere
non oicere esc

Fionanus
an Oom occcxix

meſſe ocuſ Panguʀ Bán,
cechcaʀ nachaʀ fria ſaınoán
bích a menma-ſam fri ſeilſſ
mu menma céın ın ſaıncheıʀoo

gnách-húaʀaıb aʀ gʀeſſaıb ſal
ʒlenaıo luch ınna lín-ſam
oſ mé, du·fuıc ın lín chéın
olıſeo n-ooʀaıo cu n-oʀonchéıll

cía beımmı amın nach ʀé
ní·oeʀban cách aʀ chéle
maıch la cechcaʀ náʀ a oán
subaıʒchıuſ a oénuʀán

Annal 819 AD : record # 29

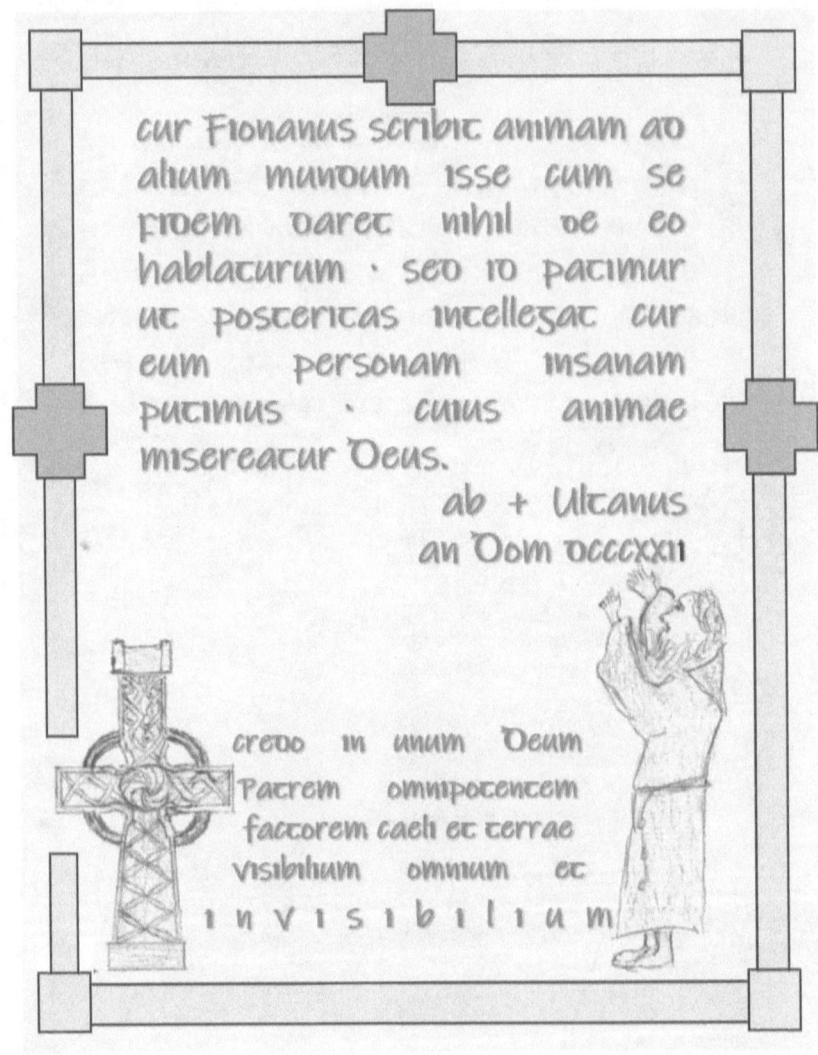

cur Fionanus scribit animam ad alium mundum isse cum se froem daret nihil de eo hablaturum · sed id patimur ut posteritas intellegat cur eum personam insanam putimus · cuius animae misereatur Deus.

ab + Ultanus
an Dom DCCCXXII

credo in unum Deum
Patrem omnipotentem
factorem caeli et terrae
visibilium omnium et
i n v i s i b i l i u m

Annal 822 AD : record # 11

Below this were the first lines of the Nicene Creed, again translated into English on the accompanying sheet:

I believe in one God,
the Father almighty,
maker of heaven and earth,
of all things visible and
i   n   v   i   s   i   b   l   e.

I was struck the apparent emphasis on the word *invisible* – was it just to fill out the line or was there some other intended meaning?

I sat there absorbed in all this. Had Fionán really crossed the boundary between two worlds in this Multi-Worlds of ours? For what seemed like ages neither of us spoke.

Luke asked the archivist if we could have facsimiles of the pages. While we had transcribed what we saw, there was so much to take in that we would really like to study it in greater depth in our own time. Also we were impressed by the graphics and the different styles of the scribes, something that would be missed by merely perusing our transcriptions. This would be possible, she said, however we would have to wait until the following day. Could we return?

Luke asked if I was OK to spend the night in Kilkenny? Of course I agreed, I couldn't even think of bowing out in the middle of all this.

That evening over dinner, we talked about the Annals and whether Fionán could have bridged the gap between two worlds. Had his story been an indication of insanity as Abbot Ultan had considered? Or was it a genuine 'other world' experience as Fionán understood it?

Reading Abbot Ultan's entry, again there was no indication that he any more than Fionán was aware of Ciarán's entry, but with a gap of some 15 years, that perhaps was not so surprising.

133

One issue puzzled us. If both Ciarán and Ultan refused to accept Fionán's story, why did they write anything about it at all?

"What do you think of it all? Real or madness?" asked Luke.

I took a few moments before answering. "I don't know. This Many Worlds theory is a bit of a mystery to me. As I understand from you, there seems to be no suggestion that crossing the boundary ever happened or indeed that it is even possible. However a quotation from Shakespeare's Hamlet comes to mind:

There are more things in Heaven and Earth Horatio
Than are dreamt of in your philosophy

"I suppose I really should keep an open mind. I find myself leaning towards believing that Fionán did have an other-world experience. He was clearly certain of his conclusion since he defied the Abbot in refusing to reject what he said, even at the cost of being labelled insane. It must have been a brave decision.

"And there is the fact that both Abbots allowed the record to stand, albeit with stated reservations. If they really didn't believe Fionán, would there be anything for us to see? Why wasn't Fionán's record excised? But when you think about it, perhaps the stated reservations were covers for their belief that Fionán spoke the truth, a belief they felt they couldn't themselves promote and defend among their peers. Their stated rejections would protect them from attacks by others, while at the same time allowing the story to remain in the Annals. What do you think yourself, Luke?"

"That's how I see it too," he started. "Even if the two Abbots did have a sneaking suspicion that Fionán spoke the truth, they still lived in primitive times scientifically speaking, and as such their natural inclination would be to reject it.

"I would say that both Abbots were very conflicted with the whole idea, but maybe, just maybe they thought, there was a slight chance that what Fionán told them had actually happened. He certainly put it up to them when he asked who did they think they were to deny God the power to make other worlds. That's why they allowed the entries to stand, albeit with their stated reservations.

"Looking at the emphasis on *invisible* in the Credo, I'm inclined to see this as Abbot Ultan leaving some hidden clue for the future. He is reminding us that the Credo requires belief in things invisible to us, which would of course include any Other Worlds that might exist. This would explain why he allowed Fionán's entry to stand."

Then Luke's eyes seemed to gaze into the distance, deep in thought. Eventually he spoke.

"As you will know from our first discussions, at the back of my mind I think, and I want to believe, that the transition is possible. These entries in the annals about Fionán's experience certainly seem to confirm for me that not only is it possible but that it did happen. How I would love to be able to transport myself back in time and actually talk with Fionán, Ciarán and Ultan."

He had another one of his deep thought moments before continuing: "But of course Killamery is only the beginning. From the annals it would seem that Saltee Island was the place where Fionán's inter universe travel was precipitated. Jimmy, we have to go there."

I agreed. I'd been having similar thoughts myself. We would go after we collected the facsimiles in the morning.

Saltee

En route to Saltee, Luke broached the possibility that by adopting a certain frame of mind, perhaps we too could experience inter-world travel. He had in mind his infatuation with the Chilean girl he had met in Peru and perhaps he had found love with her in a parallel world.

"Fionán would surely have centred his prayers and meditation at the high point on the island. This could be the location where we might encounter some natural force or other that would precipitate an inter-world experience," he said.

I wanted to visit Saltee because of its apparent central role in Fionán's adventure, but I wasn't at all taken by this idea of his. "Wishful thinking," I said, "Thousands of people visit the Island every year. Have you ever heard even a hint of a suggestion that one of them had been catapulted into another world?" He didn't reply.

Nonetheless, the trip to Great Saltee was fascinating. It is a breeding ground for many sea birds and is at the centre of a Special Area of Conservation. The island was mostly flat, but there was of course a not-very-high high point with a small cairn to mark it, just like the representation in one of the annals. We made our way there.

Luke remained at the cairn meditating, as he later told me. "I dwelt on María Inés, our meeting on the Inca trail, our many conversations. Occasionally my mind drifted to other topics, to our meeting in the Hi-B the other night, to the annals, and even back to Timbuktu, but each time, as soon as I realised, I refocused on her. But nothing." He seemed rather disappointed, as if some other world had rejected his entreaties.

Meanwhile I explored the island, looking for any remains of hermit's dwellings, but found none. Still the beauty of this isolated place was enthralling. I could readily see the attraction for a hermit.

We returned to Cork that evening. Luke took up his new position in Intel shortly afterwards, while I in time moved to Galway.

We met up on the occasional week-end. Neither of us had any other world experiences to relate and bit by bit our meetings became less and less frequent. He had his life in Leixlip and I had mine in Galway. It seemed unlikely our paths would cross again.

*   *   *

In time I met and fell in love with Hannah. I told her all about meeting Luke, his theory about inter-world travel, our trip to Killamery and the archives and showed her the facsimile of the annals.

She looked at me with raised eyebrows, particularly when I said I hadn't seen Luke for some time. I feared she was wondering whether Luke was real, and how she could make a quick escape from this mad-cap. But I'm pleased to say she did engage. She could see the logic behind this supposition of inter-world travel even if she wasn't really convinced.

A year later we were married

Fionán

Fionán was born in 782 AD and lived in the settlement at Ahenny. His parents were Fachthna and Gráine. He grew up to be an intelligent and kindly young man and showed great piety.

Fachtna was hopeful Fionán might enter a monastery and devote his life to God. He felt he had the ability and qualities to become an abbot, which would bring pride and status to the family. The monastery at nearby Killamery, no more than a half days walk away, had been founded by the renowned Holy Man, St. Gobán.

Fionán, however, did not consider that life in a monastery was for him. He was attracted to a local and vivacious girl, Bríd. He was enchanted by her fun and liveliness and was intent on taking her for his wife.

At that time celibacy was not mandatory for monks. Fachtna considered Bríd a rather shallow and flighty girl, not at all a suitable wife for a young monk and aspiring abbot. He rather hoped that Fionán would join the monastery and set his eyes on one of the nun's there, with whom he could develop an altogether more spiritual and cerebral relationship suited to an ambitious monk.

Fachtna walked to Killamery one day to speak with Abbot Ciarán, whom he knew. He explained how he believed Fionán had the qualities to be a good monk and even in time become an abbot. He also told him about Fionán's infatuation with Bríd and how he felt such a flighty girl would not be the best choice for someone destined for the higher echelons of monastic life. The Abbot agreed and suggested that he return with Fionán another day to meet him.

Fionán was clear in his mind that he wanted to marry Bríd and had little interest in monastic life. However, on his father's insistence he did agree to visit Killamery.

This had the outcome Fachtna desired. Fionán abandoned his plan to marry Bríd and decided to pursue the monastic life.

In 798 AD, just 16 years of age, Fionán walked to Killamery once more, this time to stay. Abbot Ciarán, welcomed him, showed him around and introduced him to some of the other monks, as well as to some of the nuns who lived apart.

To the young Fionán there were people everywhere. And animals. And many, many buildings, including the chapel, the library, the scriptorium, the refectory and the monks' cells. At the centre was the High Cross.

There were over 900 monks and nuns living there. They of course all had to be fed and clothed. For this there were extensive lands on which to grow food and for cattle, sheep and goats to graze. The female animals had to be milked to provide milk and cheese for the monks. Older animals were slaughtered for their meat. Chickens provided both meat and eggs. All this demanded work, in addition to a life of prayer and meditation.

Fionán took all this in as he gazed out over the land. In truth it was not that different from Ahenny, still it seemed he would have an interesting and challenging life here.

"From the start, you will join the other monks in their daily life of work, study, meditation, chant and prayer. And of course you must study the scriptures and gain a thorough understanding of your faith. When we are sure you are truly ready for and committed to our life here, you will be invited to be tonsured and don the habit of the monastery," said Ciarán.

Fionán learned quickly, fitted in well, joined enthusiastically in the prayers and chants of the monks and worked hard on the farm.

His early infatuation with Bríd never fully left him. Three years after entering the monastery and unable to rid himself of this continuing infatuation, he decided it was time to discuss his difficulties with the Abbot, who prescribed prayer and penance.

Two years later his disturbing thoughts showed no signs of abatement. Fionán had become very friendly with an older monk, Eoghan. They often tended the farm animals together. Brother Eoghan seemed to be knowledgeable on all topics and wise in the ways of the world. Fionán confided in him about his continuing obsession with Bríd. Eoghan empathised with him and at one point revealed to him his own period of turmoil years earlier. He thought at the time that living the solitary life of a hermit in peaceful prayer and meditation might help. He went to the island of Eninis for a month with the blessing of the Abbot. The experience had strengthened him in his faith and at the same time enabled him to push his conflicts into the background.

Fionán asked whether living a solitary life wasn't strange, not having the company and support of others in his daily life.

"But I wasn't truly alone," Eoghan replied. "I had the ever present company of Our Lord as well as the angels and saints, not to mention the birds of the air and the fish of the sea. Yes, it was a solitary life, but I was not alone."

What seemed to be a contradiction - solitary but not alone - made perfect sense on Eoghan's telling. "Tell me about Eninis," he said.

"As an island, Eninis is some distance off the coast, surrounded by the ocean," he replied. "There you are in a solitary existence, but at the same time in the constant company of God and his creation."

Fionán, never having seen the ocean, found it hard to visualise. "It's a vast expanse of water," said Eoghan. "In most directions there is nothing but water as far as you can see, but looking back to the north, you will see the land of Erin. It's just a couple of hours in a boat from land to the island. There is a monastic settlement nearby, Inis, where you will find someone to ferry you across."

"And do others not go there too?" wondered Fionán. "Might there be lots of monks there seeking this life of a hermit, and so negate the very solitary life he sought?"

"Some do go there, but not that many," replied Eoghan. "You will find a few stone cells there built by others over the years. You will most likely be alone on the island, but if there is another there, he will be as interested in keeping his distance from you, as you will from him. You will each be focused on your own solitary life there."

With this, Fionán began to think that the life of a hermit would surely help him rid himself of thoughts and dreams of the flesh. He went to the Abbot and sought permission, saying that he believed he would return to the monastery stronger in his faith and more committed to monastic life. The Abbot responded that this was something that arose from time to time and agreed that this should be good for Fionán. They discussed where he might go.

"I have had a long discussion with Brother Eoghan and I believe Eninis would be the perfect place to find the isolation I need in order to purge these demons," said Fionán.

The Abbot agreed. "Brother Eoghan is indeed a wise man. There in that wild and barren place he found the peace he sought. Over the years, Eninis has been a favoured place to find solitude. Quite a few monks from here have gone there for reasons similar to yours. All found it the perfect place for solitary life and meditation. There has been talk of the foundation of a new monastic settlement there, but so far nothing has happened. There are one or two hermit cells there, built over the years. It is probable you will find one empty, but if not, you can build one. In truth, it is more probable you will be alone on the island. The seas around the Island are teeming with fish, which will provide some tastey meals for you. There is not much vegetation there, but there should be sufficient to build fires to keep your cell warm and to cook some fish. It will take several days to get there, but you are young and strong. Go with God."

Fionán went to Eoghan for guidance on getting to Eninis, adding that he would spend a night with his family in Ahenny before travelling on.

"When you leave Ahenny, cross the river Lingaun and follow it south until you reach the banks of a wide river, the Suir. At that point turn east and follow the river until you come to the monastic settlement of Fiddown. You will be welcomed there for the night. The next day you must head east again until you reach the ferry point at Ballinlaw to cross another river, the Barrow. Continue east and you will reach the monastery at Clonmine. The monks will provide you with food and shelter for the night and next morning indicate the route to Inis, a short enough distance. At Inis there is a small monastic settlement close to the coast.

"After morning chant and prayers, which you will join in, the monks at Inis will arrange to ferry you to Eninis. You will make your own arrangements for the time you chose to spend there." With that, Brother Eoghan made a sketch to guide him through his journey. "Please keep this safe for others who might need it," he added.

This was a daunting trip for the young Fionán, who had never been further than Killamery and Ahenny, but he relished the prospect. He set out in the month of May in the year of Our Lord, 803 AD. Being the start of the summer, he could hope for favourable weather for the journey, and for setting himself up in his hermitage. He walked the short distance to Ahenny the first morning and was pleased to spend time there with his family. They too were eager to know how life was in the monastery. While he did not see Bríd, his mother told him that she had married another man and seemed happy in her family life. Fionán was pleased to hear this for it would now be futile for him to be thinking about her. He hoped this would make his life of prayer and meditation easier on Eninis

After Ahenny, his journey was as Eoghan had described it and he was pleased to discover the hospitality he received at the monasteries along the way. He realised of course that that should not be a surprise, since he was well used to the flow of monks from other monasteries stopping at Killamery. Weren't charity and hospitality in truth the same thing? Showing love and respect to your fellow men?

At Inis, the sight of the ocean and the expanse of sand along the coast was breath-taking for Fionán. This was all new to him. He gazed all around in wonder and amazement. The waves made the ocean look threatening and he hoped the ferryman would be able to steer the boat safely.

Next morning after prayers he set off with Brother Colm. He was very nervous in the currach with all the movement, but a couple of hours later they were safely on land again at Eninis.

Brother Colm said he would come back the next day and teach him the art of catching fish, which were plentiful in the shallow waters. He also promised to bring him some edible roots as well as a pot in which he could cook his meals. And he showed him where there was a small freshwater spring which he would need. Fionán wasn't aware that he couldn't drink the water from the sea.

The island was not large and could be traversed in a short enough time. He was alone. He found a small stone cell on the north side of the island, which would be sheltered from the winds and occasional storms blowing in from the sea. He set about collecting dried ferns to make a bed for himself, as well as some dried sticks which he could use to make a fire to cook fish, which he hoped to catch. There was a small cairn of stones at the high point towards the south western end of the island. He found a few sticks of kelp along the shore, which he made into a small cross. This he stood on top of the cairn, then blessed it *in nomine patris et filii et spiritu sancti*. This would now be his centre of prayer and meditation.

And then there were the cliffs with colonies of sea-birds that seemed to screech continuously. These were God's creatures, and as such he couldn't complain about their screeching, however he did hope they would also go to sleep at night and allow him to sleep peacefully. And of course they might provide him with an occasional egg, if indeed he could reach their nests on the cliff. Or perhaps he might manage to trap a bird, which he could kill and cook to provide a delightful meal. God's creatures they might be, but weren't they also there to serve the needs of man?

That night, thankfully, the birds did also sleep. This was a good omen for his time here. However, there was something else. Off in the distance across the ocean it seemed to him as if there was a large fire burning, not something he would have expected on a warm summer night.

The next day, being accustomed to the monastic life, he was up before dawn and ready to start his prayer and meditation. He made his way to the cairn. He knelt down before the cross and paid homage to the Lord. He started by chanting the *Confiteor* in which he begged God's forgiveness for his sins, his weaknesses and his omissions. In reality he had led an exemplary life, but nonetheless followed the monastic guidelines which held that no man is perfect and that he must not adopt the attitude that he was without failings. Indeed, the very reason he was here, his inability to purge Bríd from his thoughts, he considered a great weakness, even though he seemed to have no power over these thoughts.

After the *Confiteor*, he let his mind run free for a while, but then his thoughts turned to Bríd. He refused to entertain them and to purge them from his mind he began to chant the hymn *Gloria in excelsis Deo* – Glory to God in the highest. By the time he had finished, he felt he had a clear mind, free of unwelcome thoughts. A good start, he thought.

By now the sun had risen in the sky and the birds were waking up – the loud screeching was back. He wondered whether the ferryman, Brother Colm, might have come. He had. As promised, he had brought some roots and herbs and a pot. He had also fashioned a number of spears from willow. These, he said, could be used to catch fish. He brought Fionán to a small inlet where fish tended to be plentiful, and indeed on arrival it was clear this was so. The fish were easily visible in the shallow waters.

"Catching fish requires concentration and patience," Brother Colm said. "The first thing you must realise is that when you see a fish, it is not where you think. The water plays tricks on your eyesight and you must learn to work out where the fish actually is. The second thing is they can move very quickly, which they do when they sense a disturbance in the water." He handed a willow spear to Fionán and invited him to try his hand.

He perched himself in the shallow water, crouched with spear in hand. He kept himself as still as possible for a while. The fish didn't seem to take any notice, swimming around and brushing off his legs. Then one seemed to hover for a few seconds and with a sudden movement Fionán thrust downward with his spear. But no luck. With a flick of his tail fin the fish was gone in an instant. This is not so easy, he thought.

Colm just smiled. "First of all, even if the fish hadn't moved, he wasn't where you were aiming. It was at least a fish length closer to you and a little deeper in the water. And then, you started your attack from too high up. The fish was gone before the spear even broke the surface of the water. Try again.

Fionán tried to take note of the instructions before his next attempt. Still no luck. "That was better", said Colm, "just a little more concentration". On his fifth attempt he was successful. The fish was twisting and writhing on the spear. "What do I do now?" he asked. Colm was laughing. "Pass it over to me," he said and he took the fish, located a point on either side behind the fish's head, stuck a finger and thumb in, and in a few seconds the fish went limp. "By breaking his gills, he soon dies", he told Fionán.

After his lesson in fishing, he asked: "Why was there such a large fire burning over there last night in the summer warmth?"

"That was at Rinn Dubhán[1] where the monks keep a fire lighting all the time, to warn any boats around there to steer clear. Rinn Dubhán is surrounded by rocks and rough seas, a hazard for any sailors."

There was much to learn in this world, thought Fionán. God made the rocks in the ocean a hazard to boatmen, but he also made the monks who kept the fires burning as a warning of the dangers.

Now prepared for survival on this remote island, Fionán continued his daily routine of meditation, prayer, chant, fishing, cooking, and occasionally managing to steal an egg from a nest. Once he did catch a nice fat bird which made a fine meal.

He was pleased with the progress of his prayers and meditation and felt that he was achieving what he set out to do.

By the end of the second week he seemed to have accomplished what he came for: Bríd was now absent from his thoughts, except for the odd fleeting memory. However, he decided to remain a while longer. He had come to like the peace and solitude of the hermit's life. And the weather was kind. But he was also conscious of his dependence on the ferryman. He wouldn't outstay his welcome. Just another two weeks, he thought.

Then in the middle of his fourth week, a few days before he planned on leaving, he encountered the strangest of sensations. He saw himself in the Ahenny settlement where he had grown up, in Bríd's family homestead, together with Bríd, her father and mother, a small child and a young baby which Bríd was nursing. And he appeared to be the father! It all seemed so real. Yet it was totally different from the sort of thoughts he had come to Eninis to purge. Those thoughts were more a kind of infatuation with Bríd and had

---

[1] The old name for Hook Head, named after a Welsh monk, Dubhán, who founded a monastery there. He started the practice of burning fires to warn sailors to keep clear.

no place in the life of a monk. But this was as if it were a real other life, as if he had chosen a path to marry Bríd rather than enter the monastery. The vision, if that is what it was, seemed so real, as if it were a real life scene, as if he were a married man with Bríd his wife, a son and an infant. He couldn't discern whether the infant was a boy or a girl.

The sensation, the vision lasted no more than an instant, but he found it very troubling. It was as if all his prayer and meditation had suddenly come to naught. For a moment he considered staying on another month, this time to try harder to purge his mind of Bríd. However, he doubted he could ever forget that vision. He needed to talk about it with his Abbot. He would return to Killamery.

Back in the monastery he went to talk with the Abbot. He told him about his trip, the island, learning how to fish, his prayers and meditation. The Abbott listened approvingly to all this, then said: "So if I understand you correctly, the prayers and meditation helped you get rid of these troublesome thoughts about Bríd?"

Fionán hesitated several moments before responding: "That's a difficult question. Let me say that for a month I prayed and meditated every day and gradually my mind became clearer. While they didn't disappear, thoughts of Bríd faded into the background and I felt everything was under control. I felt I was ready to leave my solitary life and return here."

"That's good," said the Abbott. "It would be unnatural to forget entirely about Bríd. I think you should consider your venture into the hermit's life a success and I am glad to have you back with us."

Fionán looked down at the floor for several moments. The Abbot suspected there was more to come, but he said nothing, waiting for Fionán to speak. Eventually the rest of the story came gushing out.

"There's more, Abbot. Just when I was sure I was in control of my thoughts, on the very last day, when I had already decided to leave, the strangest thing happened. Suddenly it was if I was in another world. I saw myself in a house with Bríd – it was her family homestead near Ahenny – I was there with her and she was nursing a child. It seemed as if it were our child, I couldn't see whether it was a boy or a girl. Everything seemed so real. And there was an older child with her, a boy. It lasted no more than an instant, then it was gone. What can that mean? That everything about my trip to Eninis was for nothing?"

Now it was the Abbott's turn to remain silent for several minutes while he dwelt on this. Then: "Fionán, I can see why you must be troubled by this. But I think you have no need to worry. I think it was just one last gasp of your troubled mind before finding peace. I think you will find peace now. Continue to pray to God and you will see all will be well."

But all wasn't well. This image of being married to and having a family with Bríd continued to haunt him. Try as he might all summer long and through the winter, there was no relief. Initially, he spoke frequently with the Abbott, who became concerned for him. He wondered whether there might be a degree of insanity in all this.

After a few months, however, Fionán thought these discussions with the Abbot were going nowhere and he said no more about it.

Ahenny

In the year of Our Lord 798 A.D., when Fionán was torn between the pressure to enter the monastery and his own strong desire to marry Bríd, a quantum event caused the universe to split in two. Such quantum splits had happened innumerable times before, continue to happen to this day, and will continue for all time.

However, we continue on one side of the split, in total ignorance of what has happened. And of course the version that continues in the parallel universe has not even the remotest idea that you continue in this universe, on a parallel but different trajectory. Thus it was that in our Universe, Fionán as we have seen, entered the monastery at Killamery.

In that other parallel Universe created by the quantum event, Fionán married Bríd, both of whom lived in the Ahenny settlement. The two families were related but not closely, as was the practice of that time. He moved to her family homestead where he worked the land and provided for his family. Bríd's family were also tailors to the local community, so as well as working the land, he learned the skills of tailoring and spent some time making and repairing clothing in the village.

By now, in that parallel world, in the year of Our Lord 803, Fionán and Bríd had two children – a boy, Tomás, aged 3 and an infant girl, Aisling.

So it was that in the month of June that year he experienced a strange and disturbing sensation. He saw himself on an island, surrounded by the sea, and with that vision came a 'memory' of a life as a monk and a hermit. It was as if he had decided that fateful day to enter the monastery rather than marry Bríd. But of course Bríd was beside him and he could see his children. There was no mistaking that reality.

Still, he had this memory of five years as a monk in Killamery, which seemed to come out of nowhere. No detail was hidden from him. The waking at dawn, the prayers and hymns in the chapel, the hours of meditation interspersed with working the land and tending to the animals. And there was the vision of the last several weeks, making the journey to Eninis, life on the island, learning how to catch fish, and living in a stone hut.

Was this all a dream? Or had something happened? Was it the work of God or of the Devil? He told Bríd of his strange dream. She just laughed it off. "Sure I have strange dreams all the time," she

149

said. Then, after a moment: "But you're not thinking of deserting me for that monastery life, are you?"

"Absolutely not, nothing could entice me away from you, my love," he replied, giving her a hug. He spoke no more about the strange experience, but it was on his mind.

One day he thought to himself: "In this other life it seems I learned to catch fish in the ocean. If there is a semblance of reality in all this, then perhaps I can now catch fish."

A few days later he went down to the nearby river Lingaun, cut a willow stick, put a sharp point on it, and looked for a shallow spot where fish might swim. Soon he saw one. He crouched himself down, waited patiently, not moving a muscle and in a few moments he had speared and caught it. Then, without thinking, he caught the fish, put finger and thumb into the gills, and the fish went limp in his hands. When he saw the dead fish, he became afraid. "How did I know how to do this?" he thought. "I never before in my life tried to catch a fish."

Now he was concerned for his own sanity and he spoke no more about it. Yet that memory of his life in the monastery persisted. But the strange thing was that there was no further memory of anything after that fateful day when he first became aware of it. He managed to put all such thoughts to the back of his mind. And he never again mentioned the matter.

He continued to work hard to provide a good home for Bríd and the children. Then suddenly, a year later, he felt the strangest of sensations, almost as if a part of him were departing. Afterwards the thoughts of his 'life' in the monastery slowly faded although the memory never left him. Occasionally it would come to the fore in his mind, but really, he was back to his old self.

Return to Eninis

ack in our Universe, Fionán continued in his troubled mind, unable to forget those last moments before leaving Eninis. Next spring he approached the Abbot and asked permission to return to Eninis for a month. The Abbot, not having heard anything about this flash of family life for several months, assumed that Fionán had forgotten all about it, thought it would be good for him to return there for a period of solitude, prayer and meditation. "Go with God," he said.

He re-traced his journey of a year earlier. As before, he was alone and soon made the stone hut comfortable again. The cross at the high point had not survived the ravages of winter so he made a new one. He went to catch a fish for his supper and was pleased to find the skill had not left him.

He got back into the routine of prayer, meditation, chanting, fishing, cooking. While he could not rid himself of the memory of that brief moment a year earlier when he saw himself as a family man, he had, however, learned to live with it.

Then one day, in the middle of his third week on the island, the strangest thing happened. It came in a flash like a year earlier. But this time it was not just a momentary vision of a life with Bríd. Years of family life were laid out before him, even his marriage to Bríd. Everything in fact from the moment he decided to enter the monastery, a whole other world of existence it seemed. He remembered getting married; the joy of their first child, a son, Tomás; Tomás learning to sit up, crawl, then walk; his first words as he learned to talk; and growing into a fine strong boy, eagerly learning skills and helping with small chores; their second child, a daughter whom they called Aisling; Bríd nursing the infant; the infant growing up and crying at night wanting to be fed; peacefully sleeping in the afternoon; the joy of seeing her first smile; Bríd complaining of the sharp bite from her first tooth; Aisling now too learning to sit up, then crawl and take her first steps. He remembered all his working with farm animals and tending to crops and, surprisingly, learning the skills of tailoring, which was a tradition in Bríd's family. And there were the moments of intimacy with Bríd, where it seemed to him he was an intruder into someone else's relationship, but he had no power to do anything about that.

And strangest of strange, there was that time when his 'other self' wondered whether he might now be able to catch fish, and his discovery that, with no previous experience, he could!

This was more than troubling thoughts. This was, he felt sure, something real. Now instead of worrying about his thoughts, he started to wonder what all this might mean. He pondered for a long time trying to make sense of it. The prayers and meditations helped him clear his mind, so that afterwards he could try and understand everything with a fresh viewpoint. Eventually, several days later, he felt sure he now knew what had happened, and that it was no illusion.

What if, he thought, there was not one world but two. What if, he thought, following this struggle between marrying Bríd and becoming a monk, he effectively split between the two worlds. In one, he became a monk, in the other a family man. Was this possible? Certainly in the scriptures the possibility of bi-location arose. There was the appearance of the Virgin Mary in Cæsaragusta in Spain while she was living in Jerusalem. And there were other instances. But on all those occasions, the person was known to be in two places in our world at the same time. Here was something very different, he thought, two parallel worlds.

As a man of God, he wanted to be sure this was not the Devil, Satan himself, playing tricks with him. But this didn't seem to be the case as there was no element of temptation, nothing evil, at least not that he could sense.

He wondered whether it might be an illusion, his mind playing tricks on him. If it was just the single event a year earlier, no doubt that could be the case. But the sudden reappearance of the same scenario a year later, this time with far greater detail, and the memory of all those years with Bríd and the two children was not so easy to dismiss.

He thought of God, all powerful, creator of heaven and earth. Surely if he created one world, he could create two. And why should we deny him that possibility? Because this way would make sense of everything. Somehow he must have made a transition from one world to another. How that might happen, he could not say. But there were many things which happened regularly for which there was no easy explanation, yet they happened and were accepted.

He thought of the sun rising in the morning and setting in the evening. The regular cycle every year of the low sun, cold days, frost and snow in winter, followed without any doubt by spring, then summer, autumn and winter again. And there was the daily ebb and flow of the ocean which he had come to know on the island. How did all that happen? It was of course God's creation, but he must have designed rules. We didn't know what the rules were, but we accepted them. Why not therefore accept that there might be more than one world? And that perhaps it might sometimes be possible to pass from one to the other and back. Not the full physical person, for it was clear that he was here in this world all the time. But perhaps our mind or soul, spiritual and devoid of substance as it is, could be in two worlds at once. That would explain everything.

There was one more thing he needed to confirm before he could state with certainty that he had in fact moved between worlds. Since his 'other self' found he could now fish based on Fionán's transferred mind, he wondered whether he had acquired some skill while in the other world. He thought of the lives of ordinary people and soon concluded that there was no real difference between his daily life and that of the ordinary family man. Except that in the other world he had become a skilled tailor.

He thought a lot about this. If indeed he was now, suddenly and with no previous experience of the trade, a skilled tailor, surely that would convince the Abbot? He couldn't now see how his explanation could be rejected.

Still, he wondered how the Abbot would accept this. Would he be able to convince him? Or would the Abbot and the other monks now turn on him rather than accept his strange explanation? He would soon find out.

When he returned to Killamery he didn't immediately go to talk to the Abbot. He feared what might be the consequences for him if he wasn't believed. And he wasn't at all sure he could convince the Abbot of his explanation. There was something he needed to do first.

Some of the monks at Killamery were experts at tailoring and provided their services to all the other monks. Now he went to that building in the monastery where a small group of monks made and repaired items of clothing. They did not know Fionán other than having seen him around, but one of the group asked if he was there to learn and work with them. He replied that he was merely there to see what went on. They invited him to join them for a while, suggesting he 'try his hand' at working with them. This was exactly what he had hoped for and he joined in. He soon surprised the others with his skills, but more particularly he surprised himself. This new skill acquired, which he had never before tried, must convince the Abbot. He didn't have long to wait before the Abbot sought him.

"How did the month on Eninis go this year?"

Fionán thought for a while before replying: "It went very well, Abbot," he said. "But there was a very strange and intriguing as well as disturbing finale. You remember I told you last year about that brief vision I got just before I left, when I saw myself with Bríd, married with two children. It seemed very strange and at the time

154

you dismissed it as just one of those inexplicable notions which can come into one's mind occasionally, as a last gasp before finding peace. But this year something even stranger happened.

"I was meditating when suddenly this vision appeared again. But this time it was something totally different. It wasn't just a fleeting glimpse of some life that I might have lived had I married. Rather, it was a very definite memory of marrying and living with Bríd, having children and the many other ordinary things that happened.

"The two children I saw last year have names. the boy, now nearly 4 years of age, is called Tomás and the young baby is Aisling.

"Last year you will remember I spoke of seeing an infant, perhaps a few months old. Now I saw the infant was a girl called Aisling. I saw her learning to sit up on her own, then crawl. And it was all so real. I could see her taking her first steps then falling down, then getting up to take a few more steps, than falling down again. This was not just a fleeting glimpse.

"And Tomás, I remember him helping me to do various chores around the place. He was quick to learn and always eager to help out.

"Then Bríd. Always tired from minding the baby and all the other things a mother does. At times she was irritable, but then we seemed to have good times as well, able to laugh together. And it's not just that memory that day. It remains part of me. I remember those things just as I remember praying and working with my fellow monks"

He told the Abbot about all his memories, with one exception. He omitted any detail of his romantic and conjugal memories. He simply felt unable to mention it and felt it would be wrong to relay these private memories, that he would somehow be betraying Bríd, even though the experience was from another world.

The Abbot replied, not at all accepting Fionán's 'memory' explanation: "That is all a very interesting story. But maybe you are really re-imagining in this so-called memory what you encountered in Ahenny when you called to see your family en route. Did you see or meet Bríd when you were there?"

Surprised at this question, Fionán replied: "No, I neither met nor saw her. But my mother did tell me about her, that she is now married with three children, all girls. I don't see how that could have anything to do with what I experienced, Abbot."

Abbot Ciarán was quiet for a moment before continuing: "Be that as it may, your talk of your story as a real memory I cannot accept. We live in this one world created by God our Father in Heaven. There is no 'other world'. What you have told me is pure invention, either deliberately false or as a result of madness. I am reluctant to believe that you would deliberately have made up this 'story' or 'memory', since I have always known you as an honourable man.

"I am therefore concerned for your sanity. I partly blame myself for encouraging you to live a solitary life. I think perhaps you did not have the necessary resilience in yourself to cope with the loneliness and isolation, living all on your own, with no one to talk to, no social engagement. It is the natural state of mankind that everyone needs to have the company of others. Only a few can live the life of the hermit and truly deal with all the consequences of loneliness and isolation. Fionán, it is now clear to me that you are not such a person."

The Abbot sat back, deep in thought, while Fionán pondered how he might reply. Fionán was first to break the silence.

"Abbot," he started, "I understand what you are saying and your motivation for saying it. I have no doubt everything you say is solely in my best interests, and I respect that.

"However, I believe you are wrong and if you let me explain, I think you will agree with me."

The Abbot raised his eyebrows, then stretched out his hand, palm up, and nodded for Fionán to proceed.

"First, let me say that I am extremely conscious of the risks in relating this experience. I have dwelt at length on the possibility that this might be the work of the devil, however I can find nothing in my experience so far which would indicate any enticement to evil.

"Furthermore, I was very nervous about telling you this story for the very reason that you might question my motive, my sanity. You must surely understand that I didn't lightly decide to tell you this, rather it was in the belief that I was duty bound in honour and in Christ to be fully open with you.

"I realised you might say that suggesting there is a parallel world, is in itself the work of the devil. It is true that it suggests a creation which is not within our system of beliefs, but our belief system has never been cast in stone. There have been synod after synod discussing many elements of our faith, bringing new understandings. These have enriched our faith and religion. I do not see the emergence of a new dimension to be discussed, debated, resolved, poses any threat to our faith, or in any way suggests the involvement of the devil.

"As to my sanity, I have thought long and hard about this. You may respond that a man cannot adjudicate on his own sanity and in this there is a certain truth. But it is not universally so. My experience, my memories have not been subject to any variation. I am quite sure of my memory of all those events from this alternative world since the time I made the decision to enter the monastery. The memory stops exactly at the point of the recent incident. All this is entirely consistent with my belief that my own mind was projected into a parallel world for a limited time. It is quite troubling to deal with, but that is what I believe happened and I must live with it.

"There is one further thing," he said, and he related his experience in the tailoring room.

"You may ask why God Our Father in Heaven would create a parallel world. This indeed remains a mystery to me. But there are other mysteries in our beliefs and we accept them. God Our Father, creator of Heaven and Earth is all powerful and who are we to declare that his power does not extend to creating other worlds? I can find no other explanation."

Now the Abbot sat silent for several moments. He thought to himself that Fionán's arguments were well put, and quite convincing. But that did not mean that he could accept them. For to accept them would commit him to defending and promoting them. And this would surely lead to a synod to resolve the matter. He had no doubt how that would go. There was no chance any other abbot or bishop in Ireland or anywhere else throughout Christendom would accept the thesis. He would be exposed; his own position, even his own sanity would be questioned. He could not publicly accept Fionán's explanation.

He spoke: "Fionán, what you have said on one level seems very convincing and I do not doubt your honesty and sincerity. However, I am sure you are mistaken. It would indeed be a matter of the utmost gravity to promulgate this suggestion of yours that there are two or more worlds. I simply cannot allow it.

"This talk of having acquired tailoring skills is meaningless. It just means you are a natural tailor, as some men are.

"Here's what I demand of you: You must promise never to talk of this two worlds idea of yours ever again, not to any of the Brothers or Sisters here in the monastery or anyone else. With one exception. I will appoint Brother Ultan as your confessor and advisor. He is a wise and compassionate man as I'm sure you know. You may discuss all your ideas with him, without reservation. All your discussions will remain private between the two of you, so what you discuss will never be revealed, not to me or anyone else. Brother Ultan will take whatever you discuss to the grave.

"For my part, I recognise your honesty and integrity however mistaken I believe you to be. Because of that, if you offer and keep a commitment to talk to no one else bar Brother Ultan about this vision of yours, I will be pleased to have you continue here at the monastery. I will not mention what happened to anyone, nor make any insinuation as to your sanity. However there is no question of you ever being given permission to leave the monastery to go to Eninis or anywhere else for peace and solitude, for the life of a hermit. Can you give me your agreement to this?"

Fionán remained silent while he took in what he just heard. It was devastating to think he must never talk about this again. But he also knew that not to agree would lead to a disaster for him. Without the support of the Abbot, which he had thought might be forthcoming, he would be ridiculed and branded as insane. He saw that he had no option but to agree. "I accept your proposition, albeit with a heavy heart," he replied after several moments.

But for all the Abbot's renouncing Fionán's account, he did continue to harbour the thought that maybe, just maybe, Fionán had stumbled on to something. He decided to write a brief account in the Annals, including his own rejection of Fionán's account. This would at least mean that the account would be available for others to consider at some future date. He had in mind what Fionán had said, *'It is true that it suggests a creation which is not within our system of beliefs, but our belief system has never been cast in stone.'*

Insane

Fionán kept his side of the bargain. He met regularly with Brother Ultan, a gentle and compassionate man, who listened intently to everything. While he never chided Fionán for what he said, neither did he accept his proposition. He offered various explanations, none of which Fionán found satisfactory.

Fionán noticed over time that there were no new memories about life with Bríd following his time on Eninis. He wondered about this and tried to make sense of it. But the more he thought about this, the more it seemed to reinforce his belief that his mind had travelled to another world. And returned. Because if it never returned, how could he get the memories from that other world? His mind, or rather a duplication of his mind, must have travelled to the other world at the end of his first time on Eninis, and returned with all those memories a year later. Now that seemed to make sense to him.

He began to wonder about that 'version' of him in the other world. He must surely have wondered what was happening when he was suddenly in possession of years of memories as a monk. It was all very confusing and troubling. Nonetheless, he got comfort from the monastic life of prayer, work, chanting and meditation.

Some 15 years later, Fionán was now in his middle years, one of the scribes in the monastery died and the Abbott asked him if he would like to work in the *scriptorium* where the scribes carried out their work. He would and he was pleased at the opportunity for he felt he had the linguistic, the artistic and the calligraphic skills necessary. The work involved transcribing sacred texts, sometimes translating from Latin to the vernacular, and writing the annals. The annals were a series of records of notable events in the life of the monastery, the most interesting part of a scribe's duties.

Since these annals were rarely if ever looked at – they were deemed to be records for future generations to know about the monastery – Fionán had an idea. He could write about his experience here. It would in all probability remain unseen until long after his death, and at some unknown future date his experience would be revealed. Perhaps it would be a more enlightened time when such ideas could be accepted. In any case it was the only possibility he had of making his experience known. He had given his word to the Abbot that he would not talk to anyone about his experience, however this would not be talking. A fine point which was likely to be lost on the Abbot if he ever found out. Still he decided to risk it.

All was well. Three years passed, then in 822 AD Abbot Ciarán died. Brother Ultan was selected as the new Abbot. One day, not long after his installation, he came to visit the scribes to review their important work. As he perused the annals, he saw Fionán's entry asking why no one believed him.

Ultan was not pleased. He summoned Fionán and asked him to explain himself. Fionán knew he was now in serious trouble, yet he answered defiantly.

"Abbot Ultan, I can understand that you are not happy. I promised never to talk about my experiences and I haven't.

"Going back to my original discussions with Abbot Ciarán, I felt sure at the time that he wanted to believe me, but that he couldn't promulgate this with his peers without being ridiculed. I'm convinced he had more than a suspicion that I might have been right.

"I would also say that in all my discussions with you, while you never hinted at any support, you did on occasion convey the sense that you saw some validity in my explanation. In particular you gave this impression when I referred to the Credo which we recite daily:

I believe in one God,
the Father almighty,
maker of heaven and earth,
of all things visible and invisible.

"In this we reconfirm daily our belief that God created things which are invisible to us. Might not the existence of another world be one such invisible thing?

"In writing of my experience in the annals, I was not in breach of my covenant never to speak of it. These annals are rarely reviewed so I believed that it would be several generations hence before they came to light. At that time, who knows what further revelations there may be in our understanding of the world, and it would be important for evidence such as mine to be recorded. Even as I wrote, my belief as to what had happened became stronger. I have no regrets, and I hope you will accept my honest and conscientious approach to seeking the truth in this matter."

Although Abbot Ultan was caught unaware by the strength and passion of Fionán's argument, like Ciarán before him he knew he could not accept it. Instead, he replied sternly, rebutting Fionán's case.

"You may well think that I at some level saw truth in your story. But that is of no consequence. Your hair-splitting rationale for allowing yourself to write what you did, is just that. Your excuses carry no weight with me. You have transgressed, and I consider this deliberate transgression in seeking to communicate this incredible tale of your travel to another world to be an act of madness. I have no option but to declare you unfit to continue as scribe by reason of your insanity.

"I will not banish you from the monastery, rather you will continue your life of prayer, meditation and work. At your age it would be an act of cruelty to banish you. Where would you go? What would you do?

"But make no mistake, if I ever become aware of your talking about this again, or writing about it, or attempting to communicate it to another person in any way, you will leave the monastery, and you will live with the consequences.

"Do I have your absolute agreement?"

Fionán was devasted, but at one level at least relieved that he would not be thrown out. "You have my absolute and unreserved agreement, Abbot Ultan."

Fionán took his experience to the grave.

But that wasn't the end of the matter. Fionán was correct in his belief that Abbot Ultan, just like Abbot Ciarán before him, did have an inkling that there might be some truth in his story. But also, just like Ciarán, he knew his chances of convincing his peers to accept it were nil. That being the case, rather than excise the entry from the Annals, he would allow it to remain unchanged and would enter his own rebuttal. This would have the effect of preserving Fionán's entry for future generations to read, while he himself would be protected by being seen to have renounced the whole idea.

He knew that the chance of anyone reading back through the Annals was remote, and that Fionán was unfortunate in that he, Ultan, had discovered the entry.

*   *   *

Neither Fionán nor Ultan were aware of Ciarán's entry some 18 years earlier. Thus it was that the records of Ciarán, Fionán and Ultan were preserved in the annals and available for perusal by Jimmy and Luke in the Monastic Archives Museum in Kilkenny in the Year of Our Lord 2009.

Luke's Story

I hadn't really expected to meet Luke again, however circumstances were to dictate otherwise. One evening about three years after we had last met, I got a call from him out of the blue. He wanted to meet me. I sensed an air of desperation in his voice and immediately said yes. We would meet that Friday evening in The Quays, a pub in Galway.

When I told Hannah about the call, she was intrigued that she might now meet the mysterious Luke. When I explained that he sounded very distressed, we agreed it would be best if I went on my own this time.

Luke arrived just as I was entering the pub. He looked shattered. We shook hands and I said it was great to see him again. We sat down with a couple of drinks and Luke started talking.

"No doubt you remember our trip to Great Saltee Island. I remember musing: 'Since Fionán's experience of travel to another world seems to have happened on Great Saltee, might we also have a similar experience?'

"You were not convinced, and told me so. 'We're going to be there for an hour or two, like the hundreds or thousands of visitors to the island every year. Have you ever heard even a scintilla of a suggestion that anyone had had such an experience after their visit?', you said. I replied saying that you were probably right, that it was just a wild notion of mine. Still, I thought that if it happened to Fionán, it could happen to me.

"On the island, you went off wandering around to see whether there might be any remains of monks' cells, while I dallied around that cairn, lost in thought. I was thinking about a Chilean lass I had met in Peru, Maria Inés, in the vague hope that if I did have an other-world experience, it would be to a world where she and I had fallen in love. When I told you, you were unimpressed. 'That's rather wishful thinking,' you said."

I was pretty certain he hadn't come to meet me just to reminisce, but I said nothing. After a few moments when he seemed to be deep in thought, he continued.

"A couple of days ago, just before I called you, all of a sudden my mind went wild with a swirl of weird thoughts and apparent memories. I couldn't figure what was going on. I thought I must be having a nervous breakdown. It started with what appeared to be a flashback to my time in Bamako some four or five years earlier. I could see the town, glimpses of some of the people I knew, an image of Ibrahim, the man with whom I had gone to Timbuktu; but also jihadis with rifles pointing. Some of those scenes were reminiscent of my time there. I knew from news reports about jihadis in Mali, but that was all after my return from there. But now I could clearly see them in my memory."

His voice was becoming ever more distressed and his face more haggard, even as he continued: "Suddenly it came to me. This must have come from my dallying in Great Saltee. That yes, I had made that transition to another universe, not one I had dreamt of, a life of love in Chile, rather, I was back in Mali. I should have known I couldn't just pick and choose. I got more than I bargained for.

"Bit by bit a more complete picture seemed to emerge and it was horrific. I realised this was the repatriation I had spoken about that night we first met in the Hi-B. I mused about the difficulty someone would have in relating an other-world experience to friends, but if it ever happened to either of us I said, we would have one great advantage: we could talk to one another. I had to talk to you.

"In that parallel world it seems I did take up a second three year contract in Mali. For most of the time it was more or less a continuation of my first term. But all that changed in 2012.

"Jihadis were sweeping through the country and were bearing down on Timbuktu. They were not welcomed by the locals, but they were heavily armed, more than a match for the Mali armed forces, initially at least.

"You may remember I told you about visiting Timbuktu with Ibrahim in 2009. He was a bit of a wheeler-dealer, always finding some way of making a few bob. Just like that first time he again had some solar panels and batteries to deliver there. He asked if I would go with him to help out if needed. He also intended to bring an uncle and two cousins with him who were going to visit other family relations. He had travelled this route a few times recently and had occasionally met some jihadi road blocks, but they always let him through, never searched him. I wasn't quite sure whether he had some contacts among or sympathy with them, which might have explained his ease of passage.

"The volunteer agency had no problem about my going away for a number of days, but they did ask whether I was sure I would be safe. I trusted Ibrahim and said yes.

"En route Ibrahim told me of the priceless documents and manuscripts in public libraries and private collections in Timbuktu which would be at risk of destruction were the jihadis to get their hands on them. The fear was that they would see many of them as blasphemous and burn them. Many local people and officials were concerned about this and decided the best plan would be to remove the documents from Timbuktu altogether for safe keeping. [1]

"They applied for funding from UNESCO, who expressed concern for the safety of the documents. They couldn't fund smuggling of rare treasures. Perhaps they would be stolen for private sale and be lost to the public forever. There was dismay at

---

[1] See *The Book Smugglers of Timbuktu* by Charlie English, published by William Collins in 2017.

this. Some people managed to find funds elsewhere to properly pack the documents and facilitate their removal to a place or places of safety, pending return at some later stage. Everything would be done in secrecy to ensure no word got out about what was happening. Even the funders, mostly Dutch I think, couldn't talk about it until they were sure the documents had been rescued.

"This, Ibrahim told me, was the other reason for his journey, if not indeed the main reason. He was part of a group who were dedicated to saving the documents at all costs. The solar panels and batteries provided the justification for the trip.

"On hearing this, Ibrahim went way up in my estimation, from a nice man and a bit of a wheeler-dealer to a man with a sense of history and willing to put himself at risk for the greater good.

"We were stopped three times on the way and each time, Ibrahim gestured to us to keep quiet while he sweet talked the gunmen at the roadblock.

"In Timbuktu we delivered the batteries. It quickly became apparent to me that the people there were well up to the task in hand. Ibrahim drove me to the house of a friend, Yaya, before heading out again for a few hours, presumably I thought, to collect some documents which were to be smuggled out. When he returned, Yaya treated us to a veritable feast which lasted well into the night. Next morning, it was time to return to Bamako.

"In that parallel world I didn't ask about the documents. I assumed if Ibrahim wanted me to know, he would tell me. But I felt sure he did have some hidden somewhere in the truck. Probably the less I knew, the better. I hoped for a return journey as smooth and incident free as our travel there. But it wasn't to be. Ibrahim's luck, or rather mine, ran out.

"Some 300 km into the journey home, we were stopped at a roadblock. As before, Ibrahim gestured for the rest of us to stay quiet and let him do the talking. This time things did not go according to plan. It quickly became apparent that Ibrahim was unable to smooth-talk those manning the roadblock. Guns were raised and we were all ordered out of the truck.

"The one who seemed to be in charge descended on me and ripped off my head and face covering, revealing of course a foreigner. I immediately got a blow from the butt of a rifle which knocked me to the ground. He shouted something which I didn't understand. Ibrahim tried to intervene but was told to shut up - even if I didn't understand the words spoken, the intent was clear enough. Next thing I was bundled into the back of another truck at gun-point. Again, Ibrahim tried to intercede for me, but all he got for his troubles was a blow to his side from the butt of a rifle.

"The others at the roadblock descended on his truck and searched it from top to bottom. From what I could see, they didn't seem to find anything. Then he got an obvious instruction to get back in his truck and keep going. The truck I was in headed in another direction, I had no idea where.

"We eventually came to a settlement at a desert oasis. I was pushed and shoved into an old mud walled building. It was reassuringly cool inside, but that was the only reassuring thing. I was brought to be questioned by a man who seemed to be in charge. He had a reasonable command of English. *'Documents please,'* he demanded. I showed him my passport, hoping the Irish passport would be an advantage in this situation.

"He looked at the passport, then looked at me. *'What is an Irishman doing in Mali? Why were you disguised?'*

"I told him about my work in providing solar powered electricity for his people, thinking that would be in my favour. But no. He gave some signal to the man behind me who delivered a painful blow to my kidneys, which winded me and knocked me over.

"*'Get up Irishman. We don't want your western technology here. We will live the traditional way, according to the laws of Allah. You have no reason to be here.'"* A strange enough reply, I thought, given that I had been brought there in a truck and all his fellow jihadis carried modern arms. But I considered discretion the better part of valour and said nothing.

"He then launched into a tirade about the exploitation of his country by western capitalist interests and the undermining of the purity of Islamic society, its religion and traditions. I was afraid he would ask about the smuggling of documents and I was glad I knew nothing. However the topic was never broached. He was more interested in what he could get from holding me captive.

"*'We should kill you now. But maybe someone pays money to get you back, Irishman. Or maybe a swap of prisoners. Are you a rich man? Rich family?'* he asked.

"*'Not rich,'* I replied. *'I work here as a volunteer for the benefit of your people. I just get paid a small allowance'* This wasn't going very well, I thought. Then he said *'We see, Irishman.'*

"I was locked into a small room and left there. They fed me, you could say enough food to keep me alive. The food was very much local diet, a bit hard to take initially, but I got used to it. While not my preference, it was tasty enough. I was allowed out for exercise once or twice a day. I was hardly an escape risk with hundreds of miles of desert all round.

"I was alone with my own thoughts. No one would talk to me. Any attempt I made just involved heads turned the other way – I assumed they were instructed not to engage with me. I thought I would go mad and I wondered when and how it would all end.

"To try and keep myself sane, I started thinking about all the lectures I attended in college before I dropped out. Equations were my life blood, my sanity. I would go back over Schrödinger's equation, making sure I had it correct, that I understood all the elements. And other theories and equations. Then I started this game of mental sudoku. Could I imagine a grid to satisfy the rules? You

169

have no idea how difficult this is. I would draw a grid in the dirt, but if a guard came to check on me he would immediately scrub it out with his foot. I never got to the end. But the persistence kept me sane.

"One day - it must have been about six or eight months, or maybe even a year later - I had lost all concept of time - I was taken out and bundled into the back of a truck, which took off through the desert. I had no idea where I was being taken nor why. As we sped away I heard gunshot. Was there some sort of a rescue attempt? Or was the Mali army finally catching up with the jihadis? I had no idea. I was totally blocked off from the outside world for that time I was held captive.

"The sound of gunshots seemed to get closer and I heard what I assumed were bullets ricocheting off the side of the truck. Next the driver seemed to lose control as the truck waltzed every which way. At that moment I felt a violent pain in my gut. I had been hit by a bullet. I didn't know whether I would live or die.

"A moment later I felt a piercing pain in my chest. In that very instant my knowledge or experience of that other world ceased. It seems my alter ego returned to me here in Ireland. I can only assume that in that other world, I am now dead."

Luke sat back for several moments before continuing. "I have no idea what efforts were made by my family, Ibrahim, the volunteer agency, the Irish government, or anyone else to discover where I was and to secure my safe release. Were there ransom or prisoner exchange negotiations in that other world? Who if anyone did they speak to? What response if any did they get? I'm sure they all did everything possible, but I'll never know."

Luke sat back again, exhausted.

Listening to it all, I was mesmerised. What could I say? Afterwards he told me the fact that I was there listening to him and understood what it was all about, was everything he needed.

2059

Forty-six years on, Luke's strange experience in Mali in that parallel world remains troubling for him. We started to meet regularly again and from our next meeting my wife, Hannah, joined us. She is a rock of common sense, always able to help Luke through his worst moments.

Luke also in time got married. Of course he confided in Jenny from the outset. He was nervous as to how she would react. Fortunately, he always says, she stayed with him. Occasionally when we get together our conversation turns to other worlds, but mostly late at night with drink interfering a little. Sometimes we take out those facsimiles from the archives to remind ourselves that Luke's wasn't the first such experience.

He was reluctant to talk to anyone else about his other-world experience lest his sanity be questioned. I don't doubt he was right about that. As a result, it has remained a closely guarded secret between the four of us. Until now.

Prompted by Luke, we recently took to discussing whether his story should be published, lest it die with us. We were unanimous that the time had come to do so.

First, we had to reveal the story to our children and grandchildren. The reaction of the next generation was one of wonder and disbelief. Some were peeved that this element of the life of one of their parents was kept from them. But in time they came to realise that there was good reason, certainly during their childhood years when they might be subject to ridicule if they told their friends and classmates. When exactly might have been the right time? To that there was no easy answer.

The youngest grandchildren in both families are now in their teens. They too have had the family secret revealed to them.

And now, dear reader, it is your turn. If you journeyed this far in the book, you also know the story. Perhaps you believe it, perhaps not. We are too old to care what anyone thinks. As for our children and grandchildren, the worst they will have to deal with is some snide comment, to which the answer is to ignore it. What family doesn't have skeletons in the cupboard?

Perhaps this book will encourage the odd person who might have had a similar experience, to talk about it. While I feel sure that such experiences would not be widespread, I am also sure Luke was not the only one.

How will it be received by the scientific community? I have no idea.

Jimmy Sheehy
20th July, 2059

Acknowledgements

My thanks to the many people who read various parts and drafts of this book: Dan McCarthy, David Hargrave, Michael Haugh, Robbie Robinson, Cian Murphy, Michael Nolan, Tom McShane, Mary Groegor, Brian Madden, Susan Crowley, Garreth Murphy. They highlighted those insidious typos and other mistakes which have a habit of continually evading the writer's notice, as well as making valuable comments on the stories.

My thanks to Margaret Madden for translating my English into Latin for the 'Annals' in *The Secret of Killamery*, and to Annemarie Barret for her insightful comments on my cover design.

Some background...

The three stories set during *The Emergency* are essentially true to the best of my knowledge, however I have taken some artistic licence and embellished them.

Newspaper reports in *An Invasion is Announced* were copied verbatim from archives. I remember the fair days from my youth.

The letters in *Butter* are fictitious, written to match the story as I heard it. I was in Silkeborg where my attention was drawn to the quotation from Joyce.

There are no fictitious footnotes in the book.

As for the rest, wild imagination all the way.

I hope you have enjoyed reading this book. I would be delighted to know your opinion, which you can leave on the website www.flaglane.ie.

Vincent Murphy
August 2024

You might also enjoy...

Perhaps you might be interested in some of these titles, details and reviews on www.flaglane.ie:

Goodbye Kit tells the story of Michael Kickham, a missionary in New Zealand in the 1880s, how he fought with his bishop, then spent ten years in Australia before returning to Ireland in 1899. Two years later he left for an undisclosed destination. In 1908 his family discovered he was in Buenos Aires, no longer a priest. He died there in 1909. The book is written as an imagined autobiography and is based on family letters as well as extensive research in Church and newspaper archives.

Conor OBrien – Sailor Extraordinaire is a biographical account of the interesting and diverse life of Conor OBrien (*sic*, he wrote his name without an apostrophe).

1923 - 1925 he circumnavigated the globe in his own design 42ft ketch, *Saoirse*. For this he was awarded *The Royal Cruising Club Challenge Cup* in 1923, '24 and '25.

He was involved with Erskine Childers running guns for the Irish Volunteers in 1914, OBrien in his earlier yacht *Kelpie*. He was a keen and experienced mountaineer - he climbed with, among others, George Mallory who died on Everest in 1924.

Both *Saoirse*, in which he sailed around the world, and *Ilen*, which he delivered to the Falklands / Malvinas, have been restored / rebuilt in recent years and are now sailing the seas once again.

Crazy Daze – a bipolar odyssey is Declan Gould's autobiographical account of his of many episodes and adventures while afflicted by the bipolar condition. He takes the reader through his times in Ireland, USA and Zimbabwe. He writes in a humourous, open and honest style, revealing his true inner self.